Merry Mistletoe Wedding

A SWEET PARADISE RESORT CHRISTMAS NOVELLA

HOPE AUGUST

HOPE AUGUST INC

Hope August Inc
Cedar Park, TX

Cover Design by James, GoOnWrite.com

ISBN: 978-1-960048-02-8 (ebook)
ISBN: 978-1-960048-05-9 (print)
ISBN: 978-1-960048-12-7 (audiobook)

Newsletter

Let's stay in touch! Sign up for my newsletter at www.hopeaugust.com. Get early access to new releases, limited-time giveaways, and more.

Chapter One

Ansley dug her keycard out of her pocket as she headed for the elevator of the infamous Sweet Paradise Resort. Kate hadn't been lying when she'd said this resort was to die for. Ansley had only checked in thirty minutes ago, and already, she couldn't wait to start looking around.

The ice-skating rink outside practically called to her. Kate and Liam's wedding rehearsal dinner would be in a few hours, but until then, she fully intended to take advantage of the amenities this place had to offer. She couldn't remember the last time she'd been ice-skating, and she itched to stretch her legs after the long flight from Maine to Colorado.

Of course Kate wanted to get married where she fell in love with Liam. Who could blame her? After her previous fiancé had left her a little more than a year ago, Kate deserved to have the perfect wedding. So after the rehearsal dinner, Ansley was fully prepared to make that happen. She was going to be the perfect maid of honor.

Ansley slipped her keycard into the reader of her hotel room and headed inside. She just needed her coat, and then the real fun would begin. She stood inside the hotel room, her gaze sweeping through it until it landed on her coat, where it sat on the desk chair.

She hurried across the room but paused in front of a large mirror that hung over the desk. She pressed her pink lips together, smoothing the gloss she'd applied when she'd landed at the airport. Turning, she continued toward her luggage and grabbed it but then froze. Slowly, she bent to look at a suitcase that wasn't hers. The black bag resembled every other suitcase that had come through the conveyor belt at the airport, but this one had a single red ribbon tied to the handle.

Her eyes narrowed, and she backpedaled to find that her suitcase was, in fact, where she'd left it: beside the window and partially hidden by the bed. Someone had been in her room. Kate hadn't mentioned that she'd be sharing a room with anyone. Yes, there were two beds, but Kate knew how much Ansley valued her privacy. It was the reason Kate had offered her a room to herself. Maybe something had changed.

The hairs on the back of her neck stood on end as the distinct sound of running water hit her ears. She hadn't noticed that someone was actually in the room with her. She dropped her coat back on the chair and inched toward the bathroom. Just as she made it to the door, the water was shut off.

Good. Her mystery roommate was done, and together, they could sort out what had happened.

The door opened, and a billow of steam puffed from the bathroom. A man she'd never met before emerged, a towel wrapped around his waist.

Ansley yelped and spun around. She heard some shuffling sounds as, she assumed, the man retreated into the bathroom, and the door slammed shut. She peeked over her shoulder, her hand covering her mouth. Her eyes darted around the room. Something wasn't right. It wasn't the room; her belongings were here. She hadn't accidentally let herself into the wrong one.

She edged closer to the door and rapped. "Hello?"

He cleared his throat. "You're still here?"

The corners of her mouth twitched. "Of course I'm still here. This is my room."

"You're mistaken. This is my room."

She leaned against the door and folded her arms. "Seeing as I'm the one out here with my luggage and fully dressed, I don't think you have any skin in the game."

He went silent.

"Okay, so there has obviously been some kind of mix-up. I'm sure if we go down to the front desk, we'll be able to get this sorted out."

"Yeah. You go do that."

Ansley huffed. "Yeah, right. Like I'm going to leave

all my stuff here with you. For all I know, you're some weirdo who likes to smell women's undergarments."

"Did you really just say that?" His incredulous tone only caused her smile to widen further.

"Come on. Get dressed, and we can go down to the lobby together."

"With all due respect, I'm not coming out until you leave."

Ansley rolled her eyes. "Fine. I'll be out in the hall. You've got ten minutes." She shook her head. Kate was going to just *love* this.

To the guy's credit, he only took five minutes. The door to the hotel room opened, and he stepped out, wearing a pair of navy sweats, a fitted white T-shirt, and a pair of Vans slip-on shoes. His black hair was still wet, and it looked as if he'd only run his fingers through it before coming out. His gray eyes landed on her, more confident than she expected considering their first interaction.

Her mouth went dry. He was totally her type. He was clean-shaven, showing off the sharp angles of his jawline. The muscles in his arms rippled as he crossed them over his chest. He was tall—a good head taller than her.

She shook off the shock that was probably written all over her face. No one was that perfect. He probably lived with his parents or was some self-proclaimed entrepreneur who lived paycheck to paycheck. Looks weren't everything. Her parents were both attractive and had perfect jobs, and even they couldn't make it work.

Ansley swallowed, but it did nothing to alleviate the lump in her throat. She shoved her hands into the back pockets of her jeans and jerked her chin toward the elevator. "Let's figure out what happened. I'm sure we were just supposed to be on different floors or something."

One side of his mouth quirked up, but he didn't say anything. He followed her toward the elevator. She could feel his eyes as if they were drilling into the back of her head, and it made her itch to spin around and tell him to quit staring. But that would make her seem crazy, and she wasn't crazy.

They got to the elevator, and she pushed the button, refusing to look him in the eye.

"So, why are you here?" His voice was husky, low, as if he was teasing her.

She blew out a puff of air. "Does it matter? Once we get this sorted out, we won't see each other again."

"You don't know that."

"Oh, but I do. My week is going to be incredibly busy. I'm helping a friend with something, and today is the only day on which I don't have every hour planned out."

He arched one brow. "Oh. You're one of *those* women." The elevator doors slid open, and he stepped inside before she had a chance to shoot a retort in his direction. "You coming?" he called.

She scurried onto the elevator and faced him, her arms folded. "Just because I know how to run a schedule doesn't mean I'm some frigid woman who—"

He chuckled, lifting both hands. "Who said you were frigid? I didn't."

Her mouth dropped open. "You put words in my mouth."

His gaze dipped to her mouth. "No, but maybe I'd like to."

Ansley gasped. "I think I preferred you in your towel—"

He wagged his brows. "I'm sure you do."

Her face flushed crimson. "What I was going to say was that I preferred you in your towel, *cowering* behind that door." The man was infuriating. Somehow, he'd flipped everything around and stolen every ounce of power and control she'd felt she had when they'd first met. Thank goodness he would be out of her hair within the next few seconds. She didn't think she'd be able to deal with him one minute longer.

Chapter Two

I t had been a surprise to find a beautiful woman in his hotel room but not one Zane regretted in the least. She was clearly someone he would love to go toe-to-toe with. She had just enough fire about her to make her interesting. Combined with how easy it was to tease her, he could see himself spending a lot more time with her and even enjoying it.

Too bad he had that two-date rule.

Then again, their situation wasn't a normal one. He was only here for a week, and then he wouldn't ever see her again. That was what his two-date rule was all about. No one in their right mind wanted to be tied down to someone for the rest of their life. His own mother had taught him that from a young age. In the end, everyone left.

He leaned against the wall of the elevator and studied her as she fumed. He could practically see the steam rising off her shoulders. Her shoulder-length blond hair was perfectly curled and styled to accentuate her neck.

Oh, was he a sucker for that. He eyed her as she gathered her hair and twisted it over her shoulder. Her perfect pale skin practically glowed except for a tiny black beauty mark near her shoulder. She resembled a ballerina more than anything else.

Zane shoved that thought aside. He was getting ahead of himself. He didn't chase women. He'd been there, done that. It never ended well. Aloof—that was how he played the game.

The elevator doors slid open, revealing the lobby he'd only passed through about twenty minutes ago. It was empty except for the fact that it looked like an army of elves had visited. For the life of him, he couldn't understand why Liam wanted this. A wedding was one day. Why spend all this time, effort, and money on something that he couldn't keep?

Whatever. This was only one of the many ways he and his cousin were different. Liam had always been so laid-back, as if his life flowed with the current of a gentle brook. Well, except for when Sarah had passed. Zane wouldn't have wished that kind of heartache on anyone.

The woman had darted from the elevator the second she had a chance and was now charging toward the front desk. He bit back a laugh at how ridiculous this all was. The hotel was fully booked. She should know that by now. *If* there was a mix-up, it was more likely that the place was overbooked. What did she expect the staff to do?

He wandered toward the desk just in time to hear her shrill voice saying, "What do you mean there isn't another room available?"

Bingo.

She glanced over her shoulder, her cheeks red and her blue eyes flashing. If he hadn't been so amused with the situation, he might have been somewhat startled by the ferocity of it all. He forced an easy smile despite a small tremor building in his gut. Normally, he'd be the one yelling at the poor people behind the counter.

But for some reason, he was content to let her have at it. Worst-case scenario, he'd sleep on the pull-out couch in Liam's room.

The woman jabbed her finger on the counter. "I demand to speak to your manager. This is unacceptable. I was told I'd have my own private room."

"I'm sorry, miss. There are no other rooms. Between the wedding and another event taking place this week, we're fully booked. I can't even offer you any of our suites." The woman behind the reception desk licked her lips and shifted her weight from one foot to the other. "I can get my manager for you, but I promise there's nothing they can do." Her focus bounced from the woman to her computer to Zane then back to the woman.

He let out a sigh and headed over to them. "Miss—"

He peered at her name tag. "Courtney, I'm sure there is *something* that can be done."

Courtney shook her head. "Unfortunately, there isn't. I mean, there are several rooms that are available for one night at a time"—she glanced at the woman again—"but you would have to move rooms every night."

Based on the fury that continued to build behind the woman's eyes, Zane could tell that wasn't a possibility. Heck, he wasn't willing to do that either. He wouldn't mind sharing a room with her, but based on the urging coming from the little devil on his shoulder, that wouldn't be wise.

"Ansley? What's going on?"

As one, Ansley and Zane turned around to find Liam and his fiancée behind them. Zane glanced from Ansley to Kate and back. This was the Ansley Liam had mentioned a few times. His cousin probably thought he was being sneaky, but Zane could tell that Liam was trying to play some kind of matchmaker.

Zane's eyes trailed over Ansley with new interest. To his credit, Liam could really pick them. Liam might want the two of them to hit it off, but he was going to be sorely disappointed. Even if they hadn't gotten off on the wrong foot, Zane simply wasn't interested in a long-term relationship with anyone.

Ansley seemed to transform immediately. She sucked in a breath and blew it out, plastering a smile on her face. "Oh, don't you worry about a thing, sweetie. This is your week, and I'm not going to let *anything* or *anyone* mess it up."

Had she just looked at him when she said that?

Kate's focus shifted from Ansley to Zane. "What's wrong?"

Before Ansley could brush her off again, Zane spoke up. "Looks like they double-booked our room."

Kate's eyes widened. Ansley grimaced. Liam laughed.

Chuckling, Zane shrugged. "I don't mind sharing."

"Absolutely *not*!" Ansley spewed as she spun around to face him. "I'm *not* sharing a room with *you*."

Liam glanced at Kate, and it was as if a whole conversation passed between them. "Aren't you sharing a room with your brother?" he asked.

She nodded then turned to Ansley. "What if I share with you, and Zane can share with my brother?"

In that moment, Zane could see the fight leave Ansley. Or maybe it was relief. Her shoulders slumped, and she shot him a look out of the corner of her eye. It was that or share a room with him. "Yeah. Okay."

Kate's features brightened. "Great. I would much rather share with you anyway."

Courtney's voice interrupted their little conversation. "Great. I'm so glad we could get this settled."

Ansley shot her a dirty look before storming away toward the elevator. The three of them watched her go. Then Zane met Liam's gaze. "*Really*?"

Liam's brows lifted, and his eyes widened, but he wasn't quick enough to hide the hint of a smile that touched his lips. "What?" His innocent tone was anything but.

"I know what you're trying to do, cousin. And it isn't going to work."

"What am I trying to do?" Liam's smile deepened.

Zane rolled his eyes. "I'm telling you, it isn't going to work." He shook his head and headed in the direction that Ansley had taken. He wasn't sure if it was going to be him or her that moved. But just to be safe, he needed to make sure she didn't leave his belongings out in the hall as if he was some cheating ex-boyfriend.

Chapter Three

Ansley huffed as she threw her belongings into her suitcase. Today was officially ruined. She wouldn't have any time to go blow off steam at the ice-skating rink now. Instead, she'd be moving to the other hotel room and getting settled with Kate.

She loved her friend dearly, but lately, her happiness had been just a little much. It was like eating too much cake. It was sickly sweet, and Ansley needed a little break from it.

A sigh burst from her lips, and she flipped over the top of the suitcase. Her fingers trailed along the edges until they found the zipper. She dragged the little metal tab around until it was secured then pulled her suitcase off the bed.

The door opened just as she lifted the handle and strode toward it. Ansley skidded to a stop and glowered at the intruder who had ripped her room out from under her. This was supposed to be her safe haven for the week. He blocked the exit, a stupid grin on his face.

He leaned to the side, his focus sweeping through the room.

"I didn't steal any of your things if that's what you're checking for."

His steely gaze swung back to meet hers. "I wasn't thinking that at all."

Ansley huffed. "I'd like to leave now if that's okay with you."

He stepped to the side, his arms folded across his chest. "It was a pleasure meeting you, Ansley."

She froze, turning slowly. "How do you know my name?"

He chuckled. It was a deep, throaty kind of sound that slipped along her nerves and settled in her chest. "Kate said it while we were in the lobby."

"Oh. Right." She cleared her throat. "Well, I can't say the same."

He arched a brow. "You're not going to ask me my name?"

Ansley lifted her chin. "I don't see the purpose of that."

"Why not?"

His wry smile both infuriated her and made her want to stay. "Because you're obviously attending the wedding," she retorted, "and seeing as you're here this early, I assume you're also part of the wedding party." Which meant they would more than likely be spending more time together than she wanted. "You'll forgive me if I choose to delay the inevitable." She strode out into the hall and didn't look back.

"It's Zane, by the way," he called as the door shut behind her.

It took everything in her not to roll her eyes. Kate's room was just down the hall from hers, and it only took a few seconds to reach it. She raised her hand to knock, but the door opened, revealing Kate's nineteen-year-old brother. He flashed her a smile and headed down the hall.

Ansley's hand shot up to block the door from swinging shut all the way. She ducked inside then released her suitcase with a flourish.

Kate sat on the edge of her bed, legs folded beneath her. She offered Ansley an apologetic smile. "I wish there was a way you could have had your own room."

Waving her hand, Ansley wandered farther into the room. "What kind of friend would I be if I couldn't roll with the punches? It's just for a week. It will be fine." She plopped onto the bed beside her friend and pulled her legs up to her chest then rested her chin on her knees. "You just have to promise me you won't leave your stuff lying around."

Kate snickered. "Deal." She wagged her brows. "So, what did you think of Zane?"

This time, Ansley did roll her eyes. "He's too confident for his own good. And he's a huge flirt. How does Liam know him, anyway?"

Her friend shifted on the bed and lay back, focusing

on the ceiling. "Zane is Liam's cousin." Her hands went behind her head, digging into her brown hair. "He's not so bad once you get to know him. And he's seriously cute, don't you think?"

Ansley groaned as she crawled over to Kate and plopped down beside her. Their heads were together as they both looked at the faint patterns on the ceiling. "I saw him in just his towel."

Kate gasped and sat upright. She gave Ansley a wide-eyed stare, her mouth hanging open. "*What*?"

Ansley grimaced, a little laugh escaping her throat. "It was purely by accident. I went up to my room to get my coat so I could go ice-skating, and he was in the shower. When he came out..." She shrugged, her eyes flitting over to meet Kate's. "It was embarrassing if anything." Her cheeks warmed. "Not for me," she insisted. "But I think Zane wasn't thrilled about being caught like that."

Kate tilted her head slightly. A hint of a smile touched her lips, but she didn't say anything.

"What?" Ansley laughed.

"Nothing."

Ansley sat up and shook her head. "*No*, that's not *nothing*. What were you thinking just now?"

Kate lifted a shoulder. "I'm glad you came."

Ansley bumped her shoulder. "You're my best friend. Of course I came." Her features brightened. "Okay, so since we're sharing a room, we can get down to business."

Her friend let out an exaggerated groan. "Ansley—"

She wagged a finger then scooted to the edge of the bed and hopped off. "I know we have a rehearsal dinner tonight, but we should probably go over the schedule. I need to make sure everyone knows where the activities are."

Kate's eyes followed Ansley as she grabbed her clipboard and returned to the bed.

"Since most of the guests won't arrive until this weekend, it will be easy to keep things straight until then. There's a snowmobile tour tomorrow evening, ice-skating the following day, and the official dinner later this week. I have the bachelorette party planned for—"

A gentle hand landed on Ansley's knee. "It's going to be great. *Breathe*."

"No, it's going to be perfect."

"Sweetie, I'm not some bridezilla. Don't stress about it too much."

Ansley turned a surprised look on Kate. "You didn't pick me to be your maid of honor to not stress about it. You picked me because—"

"You're my *best friend*."

Swallowing, Ansley looked down at the itinerary she'd typed up before flying out to Sweet Paradise Resort. Kate might think she didn't want perfection, but what she didn't realize was that her wedding day was a once-in-a-lifetime event. It would be the foundation of the relationship she and Liam would share. A perfect wedding day meant a perfect future together. And it was up to Ansley to make sure that happened.

Ansley lifted a smile to her friend. "Of course, Kate." She stood again and headed for the door.

"Where are you going?"

Ansley froze, only two steps from the door. She forced a smile as she turned and faced Kate. "Just going to check on the reception hall for tonight's dinner." She made it through the door just as Kate's voice followed her out.

"I mean it, Ansley. Everything will be fine."

Chapter Four

Z ane wandered around the main level of the resort with Liam by his side. He clapped Liam on the back and laughed. "Dude, when you told me you had a girl for me to spend time with while I'm here for the wedding, I didn't think you meant Lilith incarnate."

Liam slugged Zane in the arm. "Ansley isn't that bad. You just haven't given her a chance."

Rubbing his upper arm, Zane tossed his cousin a dirty look. "It wouldn't matter anyway. You know my rule."

They paused in the hallway, flattening themselves against the wall to let a catering cart move past. Zane lifted his nose appreciatively. Already, he could tell the food was going to be amazing. That was one thing his cousin had lucked out on. When the cart moved into an open doorway, they shifted back to the center of the hall and continued on their way.

He glanced at Liam. "Kate is wonderful. But her friend leaves a lot to be desired. She's so—"

"Choose your words carefully, cousin. She's the one person who helped me get Kate back."

"—Miss Perfect." He would have used another, less attractive term, but the tone of Liam's voice was enough to make him swallow his words.

"I thought you liked that sort of thing."

"You and I have very different definitions of perfection. When I find a girl worthy of breaking my dating rule, she's going to be perfect in all the ways that count."

Liam tossed back his head and laughed. "What does that even mean? You realize no one is perfect, right?"

"Says the guy who managed to find two perfect women in his life. That's the epitome of luck. How did you manage to score something like that?"

Liam gave Zane a pointed look. "I wasn't looking for perfection. I was looking for someone who made me want to be better—to do better. When I'm with Kate, it's like I can do anything. And when you find that, perfection will be the last thing on your mind."

"If you say so." They walked a few more paces before Zane stopped and faced his cousin. "It's really too bad— that she and I got off on such a bad footing."

The knowing smirk that crossed Liam's face did little to comfort him. His cousin placed a heavy hand on

Zane's shoulder. "I knew you would want to give her a chance."

"Oh, I never said anything about that. I was referring to how it would have been nice to just have some fun with a girl as pretty as Ansley."

Liam's features faltered, but only for a moment. His smile reappeared. "Just don't let anyone else hear you say that." He patted Zane on the shoulder once more. "I'm going to go spend some time with my fiancée." He turned, heading back the way they'd come.

Zane glanced toward the door into which the caterer had disappeared. The smells coming from that room had been mouthwatering. He shot one more look after Liam before he slipped into the ballroom.

The wood floor looked as if it had just been refinished. Overhead, several chandeliers filled the room with a soft glow. On one side of the room was a long table holding metal containers. Every table was covered with red-and-gold-plaid tablecloths and topped with poinsettia arrangements. Each wall had been adorned with yards of evergreen garland. Instrumental Christmas music played over the speakers, making it clear that the bride and groom adored this holiday. The room looked big enough to host several hundred people, but only five tables had been set, each with six chairs. There weren't that many people in the bridal party, but the parents and other family members were likely already here.

He moved toward the buffet like a floating cartoon character following the scent of deliciousness. The selections started off with salads and appetizers, followed by the large metal containers. Steam rose from them, giving off the tantalizing aroma that had invited him into the ballroom.

Zane had just reached into the large crystal bowl holding the salad, aiming for a cherry tomato, when a ninja hand came out of nowhere and slapped his. He jumped back and spun to find Ansley glowering at him.

"You can't eat that."

"That's where you're wrong." He grabbed the tomato and popped it into his mouth with a flourish.

She gasped. "It's for the rehearsal dinner, that's why. And it's *unsanitary*." She shoved his shoulder with her fingertips, rocking him off balance. "What are you even doing in here?"

He folded his arms, appraising her. Those blue eyes flashed, and her perfect mouth was pressed into a disapproving frown. She was beautiful, there was no doubt about it. And if she weren't so uptight, she probably would have been a perfect candidate for spending time with this week.

Ansley tapped her foot. "Well?"

He jumped. "What?"

"What are you doing in here?"

"Probably the same thing as you." He smirked, loving the way she bristled.

"I doubt that." She pushed past him, her shoulder colliding with his. "I'm here to make sure everything is going according to plan."

He turned to follow her, their footsteps echoing on the hardwood floor. "I think the resort can handle its own catered event."

"Obviously not. Especially with the way you just contaminated that salad moments ago."

Zane bit back the smile that threatened to make an appearance. Ansley was uptight, but she was also a spitfire. That was something he could work with. She'd managed to make it to the end of the buffet table, and he had to jog to catch up with her.

Ansley picked up a glass near the beverages, her face devoid of emotion. He couldn't tell if she was upset or pleased with the vessel. When she put the glass down, her eyes flitted to meet his, and she frowned. "What are you still doing here?"

"I told you. I'm here to do the same thing you are."

She huffed. "If that were true, you would be checking the tables to make sure every place setting has a plate, cutlery, and a napkin. Oh, and there were supposed to be assigned seats."

He gave her a little salute, earning him an exasperated sound. Zane chuckled and wandered toward the tables. "Did you know that Liam was trying to set us up?"

Glass collided with the floor, shattering as it spread across the hardwood. Zane jumped and spun around to find Ansley staring down at the mess near her feet.

He darted around the nearest table and hurried to her side. "Don't move." He crouched and gathered the largest pieces of glass then glanced up at her. "Give me one of those extra glasses."

She fumbled for one, nearly adding it to the shattered mess before them. His hand shot out and secured the fragile cup. One by one, he placed the larger shards in the glass. "Is there a broom anywhere nearby?" His focus bounced to her once more, finding that her face had turned such a deep shade of scarlet that it put pomegranates to shame.

Zane rose. His voice softened as he reached for her hand. "Hey. It's okay. It was an accident."

Ansley's eyes shifted to meet his. She swallowed and nodded as she moved her hand out of his range. "I know." She blinked a few times and nodded again, the irritation returning to her voice. "Don't you think I *know* that?" Ansley turned in a wide circle. "There's no broom in here. You're going to have to go to the kitchen, I think."

"Of course. I'll be right back." Zane headed toward the exit. When he looked over his shoulder toward her, she had composed herself.

Chapter Five

Ansley pressed trembling hands to her face and expelled a breath. How had she managed to make such a fool of herself in front of the one person she couldn't stand? On top of that, she'd shown a weakness she didn't let anyone see—not even Kate. She'd nearly cried, for heaven's sake. The instinct to berate herself for this foolishness whipped through her mind.

She'd made a promise to herself and to Kate that this wedding would be perfect, and already, she was breaking stemware and letting her well-laid plans shatter just like the glass at her feet.

Rolling back her shoulders, she lifted her chin and shoved down those thoughts that threatened to unravel her. It was just one broken glass, not some omen about how this week would go.

And Liam could shove it where the sun didn't shine.

She wasn't a good fit for Zane and vice versa. They couldn't be less suited for each other. Granted, she didn't know him very well, but she could usually count on her gut instincts to be right.

Zane returned with a broom in hand and hurried across the room. Deftly, he swept the glass dust and broken shards into the pan. When he rose, the mess taken care of, he flashed her a smile. "Good as new."

"Thank you," she mumbled.

Her eyes remained glued to him as he strode toward the nearest garbage can and dumped the contents of his dustpan. Then he attached the dustpan to the broom and leaned it against the wall.

He turned to face her as he dusted off his hands. "What's next?"

"What do you mean, what's next?" Ansley retrieved the clipboard she'd been carrying and dragged her finger down the list, avoiding his gaze.

"I'm the best man. I can help."

She scoffed. "I'm sure you can."

"You'd be surprised at the things I'm capable of." He drew near her. "I grew up with three sisters. I can probably plan this whole wedding better than you can."

Her gaze shot up to meet his, and she gasped.

Zane laughed, holding up both hands. "I didn't mean that you aren't doing a good job, just that you'd be missing out if you didn't accept my help."

Examining him from head to toe, Ansley nibbled on her lower lip. It'd be nice to have someone else to do the grunt work—things she didn't have time to do—but if he messed up even one thing, she wasn't going to forgive herself.

On the other hand, if she didn't accept his help, she'd be doomed to having him follow her around the whole time. Her focus shifted around the room. What could she have him do?

He snapped his fingers. "Right. You wanted me to check the place settings."

Before she could comment, he headed toward the nearest table. He couldn't possibly mess that up, and it would leave her free to prepare the guest book for Kate and Liam's guests.

"Umm... what color did you say the napkins were supposed to be?" Zane's voice echoed through the room.

Ansley froze. "Dark green."

She turned to face him. He had his hands on his hips and was staring down at the table.

Zane's gaze flitted toward her. "I didn't think the blue matched the Christmas theme."

She swallowed an expletive. Fine. This would be just fine. They'd have to track down the people who set the tables, but they could get this figured out. Her lungs filled with a calming breath, and she let the hand holding the clipboard fall to her side. "I'll go track someone down."

He was already striding toward the door. "I got this."

"I don't want just any green. It has to be—"

"Dark green. Got it."

The way he tossed the comment over his shoulder didn't give her much confidence. He was probably going to show up with some kind of lime green just to mess with her. She let out a groan. That didn't matter at the moment. They'd need the jade-green napkins for the actual wedding. If this rehearsal dinner had the wrong napkins, it was less of a problem. She still had too much to check off her list.

Ansley set to work getting the guest book out. She pinned pictures of Kate and Liam with their friends on brown twine and added some red and green ribbons. A picture of Kate, Liam, and Zane caught her attention.

Her gaze raked over Zane's handsome, smiling face, and her fingers traced the image. He was incredibly attractive, there was no doubt about it—it must run in their family genes. In the picture, both Zane and Liam were dressed in suits. She couldn't help but wonder how things might have gone if she'd met him under different circumstances.

She shook her head and clipped the photo to the twine. What was she thinking? This week wasn't about her finding someone to fall in love with. That wasn't what she wanted anyway. Marriage was just another way for people to get locked into something they didn't want —like an internet service contract.

Footsteps clicked across the floor, and she turned to find Zane holding a stack of deep-green napkins. He offered her a smile as he headed toward the table. She itched to follow him over there to inspect what he'd found, but she wasn't going to feed the insanity of it all. She'd stick with her current task.

The room felt smaller, somehow, as she listened to him rustling around behind her. He didn't move much. What was he doing? All he needed to do was fold the napkins in half at an angle and place them beneath the forks. Her hands tightened on the ribbon she held. She couldn't be the crazy one.

Against her better judgment, Ansley turned. Her mouth dropped open, and she hurried to the table, where Zane was folding a napkin into the shape of a cheesy-looking tree. "What are you doing?"

He stepped back, folding his arms across his chest. "I thought these looked more festive."

"Yeah, for a holiday party. This is a wedding, or did you forget?" She plucked a napkin tree from the center of a plate and flicked it a few times until it unfolded, much to Zane's disappointment. "We just need everything to look nice. And not like some work holiday party." She folded the napkin in half then in half again and finally diagonally before placing it beneath the fork. "Fix the rest of them."

Zane tilted his head slightly. "Do you really think Kate will care if the napkins look like little pine trees?"

"It doesn't matter, because I care." Her jaw tightened. "That didn't come out right. What I meant was—"

He sliced his hand through the air. "You're a little uptight, you know that?"

Her face heated. "I am *not*."

Zane didn't respond. He simply grabbed the next tree and released it from its origami fold.

She let out a groan and stormed across the room. She wasn't uptight. She just knew what Kate wanted, even if Kate didn't know it herself.

Chapter Six

Zane bit back his grin, because if Ansley saw any hint of amusement on his part, she was likely to throw a tantrum. He'd met his fair share of perfectionists, and Ansley was no different from the others. Eventually, she'd have to come to the understanding that she couldn't always get her way. She'd have to relax if she ever wanted to be happy.

Letting go was hard, but he'd managed to do it.

Having his dating rule seemed to help. He never got too attached to people and thus never risked the possibility of being let down. He folded the dumb napkin in the most boring way. The hotel didn't even have napkin rings to make the place settings stand out.

He could grumble about it, or he could go snag some of the live branches he'd found in the kitchen. The twigs and berries had to have been left over from decorating this room, so it shouldn't get him in trouble if he took a few.

His gaze drifted toward Ansley, who worked stiffly at the table near the door. Normally, he wouldn't have even bothered fixing this stuff up. But there was something about her that made him almost want to impress her, though that thought was truly laughable. He didn't have anything to prove to her or anyone else.

And yet...

He snuck off toward the door that led to the kitchen and hurried straight for the table that had small garland branches and sprigs of berries. He'd need an armful to do what he had planned, but it would turn out so much better than boring old napkins being folded into triangles.

When he returned to the ballroom, Ansley was still diligently working on her task. He returned to his place and grabbed his first napkin. First, he folded it diagonally. Then, he brought both corners to the center. He flipped it over and brought the bottom up then flipped it once more before he brought the ends together to make what was called a rosebud but looked more like a cup with a point on the back.

Then he placed a few small evergreen branches and a berry branch inside it. Zane stood back to admire the look. Yeah, this was a better fold for a rehearsal dinner. Ansley had been right. He got about a dozen done before he heard Ansley's heels tapping across the floor as she approached again.

She remained quiet this time, standing just a few feet behind and to the side of him. He shot her a glance over his shoulder, noting the surprise in her expression. "I take it your silence is a good thing?"

Ansley huffed, spun on her heel, and returned to her station.

He chuckled. At least he was getting through to her. Maybe after all of this was over, he'd ask her out on an official date. One date wouldn't hurt. Two max, just like any other girl he asked out.

When he was done with his napkin job, he cleaned up the extra branches and waited near where Ansley was now setting up a place to take some pictures.

He studied her with interest. She was in the zone as she prepared everything right down to the last detail. Ansley was a machine. It was admirable the way she could shut everything else out and accomplish what she wanted—not that she couldn't use some relaxation too. Everyone needed that.

She stood on a chair, carefully placing a garland on the top of a stand for the picture backdrop. His focus dipped from her head down her body and ended at her feet. She still wore heels!

He stepped toward her. "Are you kidding me?"

Ansley yelped, jerking her whole body as her head whipped around to face him. Her hands flew into the air when her feet knocked the chair a little off balance.

Within seconds, he was close enough to catch her as the chair toppled completely over.

Her hands slipped around his neck, and her eyes squeezed shut as if she was bracing for impact. He stared down at her perfect features—cheekbones that weren't too sharp, a dimple that was only visible in certain situations, lush and full lips, and the longest lashes he'd ever seen. "You okay?" he murmured.

Ansley's eyes shot open, and she stared at him with those bright-blue eyes. She blinked. "What?" Her gaze searched his face, tracing his face and landing at his mouth.

"Are you okay? You nearly broke your neck. You're lucky I was here to catch you before you fell. Didn't your mother ever teach you not to stand on a chair while wearing heels?"

She scrambled from his arms, pushing against his chest until he placed her on her feet. "I wouldn't have fallen if you hadn't surprised me."

Zane arched a brow. "You don't seriously think that, do you?"

She folded her arms tightly across her chest and lifted her chin. "I was doing just fine. I'd gotten half of it done before you so rudely—"

"Saved your life? You're welcome."

"*No.* Before you snuck up on me and threw me off balance." She smoothed her hands over her dress and avoided his eyes. "Maybe you should go find something else to do so I can finish what I'm working on."

He shot a look toward what she was referring to. "You don't ever do anything the easy way, do you?"

Ansley's mouth dropped open. "What is that supposed to mean?"

Zane gestured to how she'd attached the garland to the backdrop. "You realize you could have just done this." He moved toward it and effortlessly attached it with the clips that were already holding up the decorative paper. "If you hang it low enough, it will still be in the pictures. If you attach it without the clips, it isn't going to hold up all evening."

When he looked at her, the expression she wore was a combination of a scowl and disbelief.

"Since when is a guy able to do all this stuff?"

"I told you. I have three sisters, all of whom are older than me and already married. Guess who had to help with decorating their receptions."

Her brows shot up. "You're kidding."

He shoved his hands into his pockets and rocked back on his heels. "I wish I were. But it's the truth. Like I said before, I know this stuff. You should let me help."

There was a battle of wills going on in her head. She didn't want his help. That much was clear. But it was hard to deny what he'd said.

"This week is going to be pretty hard if you plan on doing it all yourself."

Her disbelieving and perhaps judgmental look said more than words could, but she hit the nail on the head with her next statement. "Wouldn't you prefer to spend time with Liam and hit on all the women who would actually *like* your attention?"

He placed a hand on his heart and stumbled back a step. "Ouch."

To his pleasure, her cheeks colored, and she looked away.

"You're right."

Her eyes swung back to meet his. Was that disappointment he read in her gaze?

"I *could* go spend time with Liam and the others who have already arrived. But I think I'd prefer your company to that of Kate's seventy-year-old grandmother."

Ansley snorted, her hand flying to cover her mouth. She made an effort to hide how much his statement seemed to lighten the mood. "Fine. But you'll do as I say. No more winging it."

He held out his hand. "Deal."

She eyed his offering before placing hers within it. A shock of electricity sparked between them, and she yanked her hand free. He chuckled. "Sorry. I guess sometimes, I'm too hot to handle."

Ansley rolled her eyes then turned away from him to work on something else. He chuckled again. He'd been telling the truth. Spending time with her was proving to be far more interesting than hanging out with his cousin would ever be.

But Liam didn't have to know that.

Chapter Seven

Ansley glanced across the table at Zane for the hundredth time, hating the magnetic sensation that was practically pulsating from him. She didn't understand it, which made her hate it all the more. Zane was a ladies' man. She'd heard a few snippets about him already from Kate, and she'd already decided she couldn't trust him.

He was too full of himself.

So why couldn't she get her mind off him? Maybe it was because he was her own kind of forbidden fruit—mostly because she knew better than anyone that being tied down usually meant heartache in the end, and she'd gotten really good at avoiding it. There was no way she wanted to have what Kate and Liam had.

No way.

Of course she was happy for them. They genuinely looked happy, and she'd be the supportive best friend for as long as their relationship lasted. There were never guarantees with that sort of thing. Marriage just wasn't a realistic goal.

She didn't want to get married—probably ever.

Doing so meant there would be the expectation of children and a house and settling down in the suburbs. Gag. That meant no more parties. No more doing what she wanted when she wanted. No more fun.

Zane's eyes locked with hers.

Dang it!

She tore her eyes away and stared at her plate. That had to be the fifth time he'd caught her looking at him. And the smug idiot was grinning as if he'd just won the lottery. He needed to get over himself.

Ansley might have been drawn to him at the moment, but it was only because he had actually done a good job with the decorating, and he'd caught her before she had given herself a concussion. As much as she wanted the memory to leave a sour taste in her mouth, all she could think about was how nice his strong arms had felt as he'd held her close to his chest.

Stop it, Ansley. You're better than this. You're a grown woman with a career and enough brains to realize when a guy is no good for you.

She peeked at him once more. Wrong choice. Zane was still smiling at her.

Ansley rolled her eyes and picked up her glass to take a long sip, tuning in to what Liam was saying.

"We were thinking about taking the snowmobiles up

the mountain. Not very far, seeing as it's dark. But just enough that we can get away from the lights of the resort and see the stars. Are you guys game?"

"Oh, I don't think..." Ansley glanced at Kate. Those dang puppy-dog eyes worked every time. She stifled a groan. "Sure." Her tone held a sickly sweet note. Surely Kate would read through it in a second.

"Great!" Kate rested her head on Liam's shoulder. "We have to do some fun stuff before the rest of the guests arrive tomorrow afternoon. Once they're here, we won't have a moment to ourselves."

Ansley could still feel someone's gaze on her. Zane's focus was burning a hole right through her. If they hadn't been sitting with Kate and Liam at the moment, she'd have snapped at him and told him to look elsewhere.

Who was she kidding? No, she wouldn't. It was nice to be noticed, even if it was by Zane—even if she had no intention of letting him get anywhere near her.

Kate leaned over the table. "This place looks amazing, Ansley. I didn't realize you could do so much."

This time, Ansley couldn't help it. She met Zane's gaze. She might not believe in love or marriage, but she wasn't a liar. "Actually—"

"I know, right?" Zane lifted his glass and held it up. "To Ansley and her magnificent ability to turn a place like this into something even more magical." The corners of his mouth pulled up into one of his trademark dashing smiles.

Liam and Kate lifted their glasses with him, toasting all her work.

Ansley scowled. "*Actually*, it wasn't all me. Zane helped out a lot."

The expressions that both Liam and Kate wore were almost reflections of one another. As one, they turned toward Zane. Liam spoke first. "I didn't know you had such a flair for decorating." His teasing tone seemed to irk Zane, whose body visibly stiffened.

"I know a little," Zane murmured. "But Ansley gave me all the direction."

Kate's attention bounced from Zane to Ansley and back as if her eyes were playing ping-pong. "That's... neat."

"I thought you said Ansley didn't play well with others," Liam teased.

Kate dug her elbow into Liam's side, and he grunted. Kate's assessment of Ansley was fairly accurate. It was easier to get things done the right way the first time when she did them herself. But as much as she'd hated to admit it, Zane did know what he was talking about.

The only problem was how thick the air had become. Was it her imagination, or did Liam and Kate both expect something more to happen? Were they wanting some kind of confession? Because if they believed their match-making plans had worked, they were more delusional than Ansley had thought.

She rose to her feet and tossed her napkin onto the plate. "Well, I think I'm going to check in with the kitchen about the cake. People are starting to clear out, and I'd say tonight's dinner was a success."

Kate's hand shot out and grasped Ansley's. "You can't. Right after this, we're doing the snowmobile ride, remember?"

"I'm sure I have time to talk to the chef—if he's still here."

Her friend shook her head. "They said we have to check out the equipment before they're all locked up for the night, and you're not even dressed yet. You don't have time to do anything else."

"No one else is ready." It was a silly excuse but likely the only card she could play.

"Exactly. We should probably all be headed up to our rooms to get changed and meet down at the front doors as soon as possible." Kate rose from her chair. She leaned over and kissed Liam on the cheek. "We'll meet you guys in five minutes."

"Five minutes!" Zane scoffed. "What makes you think Ansley can get dressed that fast?"

Ansley gasped even as Zane winked at her. "That stereotype is so outdated. I bet you we women can be ready long before you two."

Zane rose from his chair and tossed down his napkin. "Oh yeah?"

"With my eyes closed." She cringed inwardly. What a stupid thing to say.

Zane chuckled. "On your mark."

Her eyes widened, and Kate squealed.

"Get set," he continued.

Liam scrambled out of his seat. "I don't think—"

"Go!" he hollered, causing the guests at the other tables to jump.

All four of them sprinted across the tiled floor toward the exit.

Chapter Eight

Z ane laughed as he slowed just enough to let the women get ahead of them. He grabbed Liam's shirt and pulled him back almost too hard, but Liam kept his balance. They both breathlessly stopped at the door to the stairs, and Liam faced him. "They're going to win."

Zane gestured toward the elevators. "Let them. I have a better idea for later."

Liam was still doubled over, panting, but craned his neck around to look up at Zane. "What sort of idea?" He straightened as they strode toward the elevator. "Because I don't know if you remember, but Kate can be really competitive. And if you team her up with Ansley, that's a disaster waiting to happen."

The elevator doors slid open, and they stepped inside. Zane leaned against the wall, his hands braced against the rail. "I thought it might be fun to have a snowball fight."

Liam's eyes lit up. "That's perfect."

"I know."

They made it to their floor, the only sound their labored breathing as it began to settle. When the doors opened, Liam chuckled and shook his head. "I knew it."

"Knew what?"

He gave Zane a pointed look. "That you and Ansley would hit it off. Kate didn't think it would work. But I *knew*." He took a few steps ahead, but Zane slowed, placing a hand on Liam's shoulder.

When his friend faced him, he gave him what he hoped looked like a patient and understanding smile. "Dude, how long have you known me?"

Liam snorted. "Is that a trick question?"

"Exactly. And how many girls have I broken my two-date rule for?"

Liam's amused expression disappeared fast.

"There it is. Okay, I just wanted to make sure you realized what you were trying to accomplish here." Zane moved past him, but this time, Liam stopped him.

"I saw the way you two were staring at each other tonight."

Zane shrugged. "So? I stare at all pretty girls like that. It doesn't mean I want to lock myself up and throw away the key. No woman is perfect enough to do that for. I'm sorry, buddy. While Kate might come close, not even she can fit the bill."

An exasperated groan left Liam's throat. He threw his head back and muttered, "Why do you have to be so stubborn all the time?"

"Stubborn? I'm sorry, but since when is it your responsibility to find me a woman? Besides, I'm worried for you. How can you be happy when you'll be tied down to only one woman for the rest of your life?"

Liam shot him a dark look that quickly faded into something approaching disappointment. "Because she completes me."

Zane swallowed the sarcastic laugh that almost erupted after seeing another one of those warning looks his cousin had perfected.

"She makes me want to be better, not because she's perfect but because she isn't."

Arching a brow, Zane folded his arms. "You realize that doesn't really make sense, right?"

"You don't get it now, but you will. People aren't perfect. You said it yourself. But that means you aren't, either."

"I never said I was."

"But you said you were looking for perfection. Isn't that a little hypocritical?"

Liam's words hit Zane like a punch to the gut. Yes, far back in the recesses of his mind, he had acknowledged that he wasn't perfect, but maybe that was what made not settling down so much easier than trying to find someone worth the trouble.

He shook his head. "Doesn't matter. You know what

it was like growing up in my house. People don't stick around. I'm not ready to put myself out there for anyone if I get even the barest hint that they're going to cut and run."

"But how are you going to figure out if they'll stay if you won't give them more than two dates to prove themselves?"

"There's where my plan is genius, Liam. If someone makes such a good impression on me that I *want* to see them again after two dates, then I guess they've passed the first test." He brushed past Liam without being held back this time and did his best to ignore his cousin's final statement.

"Love isn't supposed to be about tests, Zane. It's supposed to be about trust."

Liam didn't know anything. He'd found love more than once, and the first had left him against her will, although dying from cancer didn't really count as leaving. Kate was a good one, he'd admit that. But beyond a very select few, women—even men—only stayed when it suited them. His mother had taught him that when she'd left Zane's father and her four children for someone else.

But they were fighters, each and every one of them. He'd survive—and without needing to lean on anyone to do it.

It really was too bad, though.

Ansley was a spectacular specimen. She was fiery and headstrong, but every so often, she'd let down her walls to allow him to see the secret garden she protected. Her blue eyes could be as warm and calm as the waters beyond a golden beach or as frigid as the icicles that hung from the resort's eaves.

Zane shoved aside those dangerous thoughts. He was only fixating on her because she was the only one worth occupying his time while being stuck at this hotel. She was his little source of entertainment, and he'd take advantage of that until it was time to go their separate ways.

By the time he was changed and headed down toward the hotel lobby, he'd missed three calls from Jake —likely at the behest of a certain spunky blonde. He tugged on his knitted hat and strode into the lobby to find two frustrated women and their irritated companion.

Zane's gaze bounced from one to the next until landing on Ansley. She wore a white parka and blue snow pants. Her arms were folded and her cheeks flushed. Had he really taken that long to get ready?

Just as he arrived, Kate turned on her heel and headed toward the doors. "If we don't get the snowmobiles, I'm dumping a bucket of ice water on you while you sleep."

Zane lifted a brow as he glanced in his cousin's direction. "Do you think she'd actually do that?"

"*I'd* do it, and I wasn't down here waiting as long as they were. I wouldn't put it past her to get a copy of your keycard from her brother. Do yourself a favor and don't mess with the bride before her wedding day."

Zane couldn't help the chuckle that bounced around his chest as they moved out into the cold night air. A few lazy snowflakes drifted to the ground, and a set of loud-speakers started playing "Baby, It's Cold Outside."

Immediately, Kate gasped and turned around to lock eyes with Liam. She sang the first line, and he joined in.

Zane slowed, having just come up beside Ansley. He muttered out of the corner of his mouth, "Did I miss something?"

"It's their song," Ansley murmured back.

"Do they realize it's the ultimate stalker song—"

"Just let them have this moment." She picked up her pace, apparently knowing exactly where they were headed.

He jogged to catch up with her. "Are you *really* that upset with me?"

Ansley rolled her eyes. "What's the point? You're going to do what you're going to do, right? Let's just get this little ride over with so we can get back to our rooms and not have to torture ourselves any further tonight."

Chapter Nine

Ansley could feel Zane's eyes on her. Ever since their charged moment while setting up the banquet room, things had been a little different. She couldn't put her finger on it, but she was sure it had all started at that point.

Kate and Liam walked ahead of them, cuddling close over clasped hands as they strode forward. Zane was behind Ansley, and no matter how fast or how slow she made her steps, he was right there.

She made sure Kate and Liam were a good distance ahead before she whirled and faced him. "Will you stop that?"

He stumbled back a step, just staring at her like she was crazy.

Ansley let out a harsh breath. "You're acting really weird."

"*I'm* acting weird? What about you?" Zane's

charming smile made another appearance. "Seems to me you have nothing better to do than focus on what I'm doing."

"That's because all you seem to be interested in is hovering. I said you could help, but that doesn't mean I want you underfoot." Ansley spun around once more and continued to follow their friends.

This time, Zane hurried to catch up and walk by her side. "If I'm hovering, it's because I'm intrigued."

She shot a look at him out of the corner of her eye then focused on the path before them. The snow crunched beneath her boots, and the cold air was starting to seep through her layers of clothing. At this point, she didn't need to hear what he wanted to say. She'd already made up her mind about him.

"Aren't you going to ask what's intriguing about you?"

"No."

"*No*?" He chuckled. "You're a hard nut to crack, Ansley."

"No. I'm pretty easy, actually. But I prefer spending my time with people who are a little less shallow."

He scoffed. "Shallow? I'm not shallow."

"Didn't I hear somewhere that you only go on two dates with any individual woman?" She'd heard something to that effect back when Liam and Kate had just gotten together. Those sorts of rules never remained a secret for long. She couldn't even remember who had mentioned it or if it was actually true. But none of that mattered anyway. Just because Zane was handsome didn't make him someone to fawn over.

Her question put a stop to his side of the conversation. Good. Maybe he'd leave her be for a while—at least long enough to get her head on straight. And yet she felt a small twinge of disappointment that he hadn't denied that rumor. She stifled a groan. Zane was right. She was paying far too much attention to him and what he was up to.

Zane worked his jaw but remained silent until they made it to the snowmobiles. It was as if she was in a fog. Her thoughts were a tumultuous mess. She shouldn't be thinking about Zane and the way he'd impressed her with his décor knowledge. Nor should she be thinking about his dark-gray eyes and the way they could make her feel more vulnerable than she ever had in her lifetime.

Ansley shook off those thoughts and berated herself for allowing herself to fantasize about him. Zane was off limits. She was busy this week anyway. And he was a tool.

"Sounds fun to me. Ansley? What do you say?"

"Hmm? What?" Her gaze shot to Zane and then bounced to Kate and Liam. "Sure. Whatever. I'm good with it." Whatever it was, she'd muddle through, if only to be done with this ride and be able to head back to the warmth of the resort.

"Great!" Zane rubbed his hands together.

Kate's eyes narrowed. "Are you sure? Because we could do something else..." The tone in her voice made it clear she didn't want to do anything else. She'd had her heart set on this ride.

Ansley glanced at Zane. His wide smile launched her heart into her throat, but she shoved it down. "I'm fine. Let's all get our snowmobiles and head out."

Kate's frown deepened. "That's the prob—"

"She said she was fine. Don't push it." Liam wheeled Kate around and headed toward the rental shed.

Zane ducked his head toward her, and she stiffened, pulling away from him. He didn't seem fazed in the least. "I thought the second you found out we had to share a snowmobile, you would veto this whole thing. Way to be thinking of others."

She stilled. "*What?*"

"Yeah. I mean, I guess I get it. You *are* the maid of honor. It makes sense that you would do whatever it takes to make the bride happy, even if it means riding with a guy you want *nothing* to do with."

Ansley bristled. "I never said I wanted *nothing* to do with you." Her scowl left her face, and she glanced in the direction Liam and Kate had taken. Her lip came between her teeth, and she chewed on it, this fresh dilemma tearing at her. Maybe she deserved this. She hadn't been paying attention to what was happening. She knew better than to agree to anything without knowing what was at stake. But it wasn't as if she could make an excuse and back out of this activity now.

She heaved an exaggerated sigh as she pushed past him. "Fine."

Ansley picked up the pace, putting what little distance she could between herself and Zane, not caring that it would be pointless in a few minutes. She finally caught up to Kate and Liam and purposefully avoided Kate's curious gaze.

The man standing in front of their group gave brief instructions on how to steer. He gestured to different components of the equipment, emphasizing the difference between how to move forward and how to brake. "But most importantly, you're going for an evening ride. It's already getting darker than we'd prefer, so I need to stress the importance of staying on the trail. Under no circumstances are you to leave it."

"Excuse me." Kate raised her hand. "Are the trails clearly marked? We've been here before, and last time, there was a tour guide."

The gentleman nodded. "Yes. There are a few trails, and the one you are clear to follow is marked with colored lights to brighten your path. Stick to the right trail, and you'll be able to find your way back. Watch the time and be back by nine, or the gates will be closed, and you won't get the snowmobiles back into storage."

Kate got situated on one snowmobile behind Liam and wrapped her arms around his middle, resting her cheek against him.

Zane settled onto the other vehicle and patted the seat behind him. "Come on, Ansley. We can share body heat."

She huffed and rolled her eyes, every last nerve ending

on edge. The last time she'd been close enough to touch him, she'd felt a sort of spark.

Liam started his engine, as did Zane. Ansley had only one more moment to hesitate before Kate and Liam zipped out onto the trail.

Scrambling onto the back of the snowmobile, she squeezed her eyes shut as tightly as she could and wrapped her arms around Zane's middle. This felt so much more dangerous than driving a machine herself. If he were to hit a bump, she'd end up flying off. All she could do was hold on tight and pray he'd be smart.

Chapter Ten

I t was all fun and games until she had her arms around him. Zane could tease circles around her. He was comfortable with that—it was yet another way to put distance between the two of them.

But now that she was leaning into him, his heart had started racing again. His breath hitched in his throat, and he tightened his grip on the handlebars. Ansley was just like every other girl he'd dated. So why was her touch affecting him this way?

Zane fought to keep his expression neutral, but the way her scent wafted over him was making it increasingly more difficult. He shook off the strange feeling and shifted in his seat before hitting the gas.

Ansley squealed behind him, and a smirk filled his face. He called over his shoulder, "Hold on tight!"

She stiffened just as he leaned forward and accelerated.

"Zane," she screeched, "you have to stay on the trail!"

"Who said I'm not?" he hollered back.

Ansley tightened her hold on him, and his smile widened. They went over another bump, eliciting another squeal from his passenger. "Be careful!"

"What are you afraid of, Ansley? That you'll actually loosen up and have a little fun?"

"*What*?"

They came around a bend, and before them was a fork in the trail. What had the guy said? They were supposed to stay on the trail, but up until this point, there had been three different-colored lights marking it. To the right were bright red ones; to the left were orange and blue. Liam and Kate had long since disappeared, and the paths were equally packed from rides taken during the day.

His focus shifted from one trail to the other and back. He figured his odds were better if he took the trail with two different-colored lights. Zane leaned in that direction and charged forward. What was the worst that could happen? These trails were supposed to be easy enough that novices could handle them.

They sped along the trail, developing a good rhythm. Ansley's grip on him eased, feeling more like a hug than as if she was holding on for dear life. It was nice. And then a sudden thought popped into his mind.

He could get used to this sort of thing.

Zane's throat went dry, and his heartrate accelerated faster than the snowmobile they were riding.

Treachery. His heart had infiltrated his mind and was giving him the wrong kinds of signals. He wasn't a relationship guy. And Ansley was definitely not the kind of girl who would put up with his antics. They couldn't have been more poorly matched.

But his heart seemed to be hanging on to that hope, or maybe it was a need. He wanted something. Maybe not with Ansley—could be with someone else.

Why *not* Ansley?

Her face pressed between his shoulders, and he stilled, glancing back at her. As if against his own will, he released one of the handlebars and brought it to cover hers. For a split second, all his rules went out the window. He could forget that his mother had walked out on her family—that all women inevitably hurt the men they were with.

The ground beneath them dipped at an awkward angle, and the machine sailed through the air, higher than expected. He lost his grip on the other handlebar, and his stomach bottomed out as the snowmobile disconnected from their bodies. As if in slow motion, they flew backward.

The engine whirred and sputtered, going in the other direction. He vaguely associated Ansley's scream with all the commotion taking place until he landed hard against the packed snow. His shoulder hit with the most force, sending waves of pain slicing through his arm and all the way down to his fingers. The spinning world came to a stop, the starry sky overhead.

Zane groaned.

The engine squealed, and then the sound died away. Zane put all his weight on his good hand and pushed himself into a seated position. Though they were out on a mountain, a handful of floodlights had been installed for those who came out here when it got dark, so he could see that the snowmobile was on its side, half buried in a drift beside the trail. It didn't look any worse for wear. Zane surveyed the rest of his surroundings.

His heart stopped. "Ansley!"

Scrambling to his feet, he fumbled through the snow until he reached her side. His hands hovered over her body. Ansley's eyes were closed, but her chest rose and fell with a consistent rhythm.

"Ansley," he whispered, "are you okay?"

Her eyes flew open, and she sat up suddenly.

"Whoa. Take it easy. Are you hurt? Anything broken?"

Her wide eyes swept around them. "What? No, I don't think anything is broken." Her voice shook with each word that left her lips.

He fully expected her to yell at him, to blame him for their current predicament. But instead, her gaze landed on his face, and she gasped, causing him to jump.

"Your face. It's—cut." She put her gloved fingers into her mouth and bit down on the fabric so she could yank her hand free. Ansley gently touched the spot above his left eyebrow.

Zane winced, sucking in a sharp breath.

Their eyes met for a moment before she dragged her attention back to his wound. Her voice was low, almost inaudible, as she murmured, "It doesn't look too deep, but you'll want to get it looked at." Her touch was soft, and her fingertips were almost too warm against his chilled skin. Was it possible that Ansley was different? She'd prioritized him over her own concerns, and they weren't even romantically involved. That trait wasn't very common in his current dating pool, and it had him second-guessing the two-date rule he'd made for himself.

He reached up and grasped her hand with his, forcing her to meet his gaze again. His brows furrowed. "Are you *sure* you're okay?"

Ansley stared at her free hand, twisting her wrist and then her arm. Next, she checked her legs, first the right then the left. When she got to her left ankle, she breathed in sharply, and a whimper escaped her lips. Both her hands reached toward her injury. She brought her concerned eyes up to meet his. "I don't think I'll be able to put any weight on it." Ansley gingerly touched the area just above her boot and shook her head. "I *definitely* won't be able to put any weight on it. How are we going to get back?" Her breathing grew less controlled. "I don't want to freeze to death."

He placed a gentle but firm hand over hers. "It's going to be okay. I'll get the snowmobile turned over, and we'll head back. Nice and slow." He couldn't tell, but he thought he saw a tear slip down her cheek. Zane squeezed her hands and got to his feet. "Don't worry. I'll get us back."

Chapter Eleven

Ansley's sharp eyes followed Zane as he stumbled over to the toppled snowmobile. Based on the way he was limping, he didn't seem any better off than she was. He might have been seriously hurt, but he wasn't telling her.

She bit back the instinct to berate him for trying to be macho. He was trying to help them both get back.

The only problem was that if he wanted to do so, he probably shouldn't be trying to lift a five-hundred-pound machine alone. Zane made it to the vehicle, steadied himself, and grunted as he attempted to push the thing upright.

His growl of frustration echoed in the snowy mountains. Clumps of freshly fallen snow fell from disturbed branches, and he made a second unsuccessful attempt.

"It's probably wedged. I don't think it's going to work," she called. Her voice shook with worry despite her attempt to keep it steady. "You should preserve your strength."

Zane grunted again, pushing into it. "We. Can't. Stay. Out. Here." He glanced in her direction, but she couldn't see his expression. "We'll freeze."

"Someone has to come looking for us. It's not like no one knew we'd be out here." Even to her own ears, her hopeful voice was anything but. "Kate and Liam—"

"—went on the other trail. I'm almost certain of it. We're stranded, Ansley."

She swallowed hard then straightened her shoulders. "Fine. Then I'm coming to help you." She moved to stand up.

His angry shout stopped her cold. "Don't you dare!"

Ansley's brows shot up. "Excuse me?"

He limped toward her. "Under no circumstances are you to put any weight on that foot without getting it looked at."

She folded her arms. "You're not the boss of me." Fury seared her face. How dare he try to control her? They weren't together. He didn't have any say in what she did or didn't do.

Zane laughed. It was unexpected and brought her up short. He stood in front of her, his whole demeanor slightly more relaxed. "Did you just say that?"

Searching her thoughts for what she'd said, she couldn't think of one reason why her statement would have made him laugh. "Yeah, so?"

He crouched, wincing as he lowered himself. "Don't

you think you're a little old to be saying something like that? I know I'm not the boss of you. But that doesn't mean I shouldn't do my best to prevent you from making bad decisions. Besides, Kate would kill me if she knew I didn't at least try to keep you off your feet."

"And what about you? Clearly, you're worse off than you're letting on. So what are we going to do?"

Zane's eyes narrowed as he peered in the direction from which they had come. "I guess I could try to carry you back to where the trails forked."

Eyes wide, Ansley scooted back a foot or so. "No. Absolutely not."

He quirked a brow at her, his lips twitching into a smile. "Why not?"

Because that would mean there would be no distance between their bodies. He'd be close enough for her to hear his steady breathing. Close enough to smell his cologne. Close enough to touch his skin. Ansley shook off those traitorous thoughts. "Because you're hurt too. How can I expect you to carry me when you're limping? And what if I weigh too much? It'd just be better to hunker down and wait for someone to come looking."

Zane moved to within what felt like mere inches of her. "And do what exactly? Share our body heat?"

Her face warmed at his suggestion. That option sounded just as bad—or rather, so good that it was obviously a bad idea. She clutched at the snow in frustration. "I doubt we'll be out here that long."

She watched him wince as he settled into a seated

position right beside her. His arm brushed against hers as he leaned back on both hands.

"How long do you think it will take before they notice we're gone?" He gave her a side-eyed glance. "Do you suppose they'll assume we snuck off to be together?"

Ansley gasped. "Of course not. Kate knows I can't stand you."

This made him turn. His expression was unreadable. Was he upset by that statement? Did he even believe it? The way they'd been catching each other's gazes all night might have led him to assume she'd started to enjoy his company. Ansley huffed. He probably already assumed so because he was a little too cocky.

"What are you thinking?"

She jumped and glanced at him once more. "What? Nothing."

The corners of his mouth twitched. "No. It's something. The way you blew out that little breath—I'm inclined to think that you're not telling me the whole truth."

"You're a little too sure of yourself."

"I'm *very* sure of myself, I assure you." He picked up a handful of the soft snow and let it fall back to the ground. "Let's just say I can sense these things."

She huffed again.

"Say I'm right. For one moment, stand in my shoes. Do you think you have shown any indication that you can't stand me today?" He chuckled, and the warm sound washed over her, warming her right to her core. "It's fine. I have that kind of effect on people."

Ansley scowled. "Maybe I'm just really good at acting."

He shook his head. "I don't think so. But you know what I think?"

She stared at him, not willing to give him the pleasure of knowing just how curious she was about his answer.

Zane met her gaze steadily. "I think that you're scared to like me because you know we could be great together. But you also know any relationship would be doomed."

Her brows creased. "*What*? I'm *not* scared. And I *don't* think we'd be good together."

He shifted so his face truly was only inches from hers. His warm breath puffed out in little white clouds, grazing her cold cheeks and sending shivers through her body that had nothing to do with the temperature outside. "Oh? Because I *know* we would."

Ansley gaped at him. What was she supposed to say to that? Was he saying he was interested in her? Did this mean he wanted to take her on a date? Her eyes remained glued on him. A very small part of her wanted to explore what it would be like to be in a relationship—even one with Zane.

His hand came up to her face, and he brushed his knuckles against her cold cheek. His voice dropped to a whisper. "I like your fire, Ansley. Liam knew exactly what he was doing when he decided to orchestrate this whole thing."

"He did?" she murmured.

"He did. Only he didn't account for one unavoidable problem." His eyes studied her, and the soft smile he wore only added to the tremors in her stomach. "We're both too smart to let ourselves get hurt like that." Zane pulled back, his hand dropping back to his side. He focused down the trail they'd come from then glanced at her out of the corner of his eye. "Definitely too smart."

Chapter Twelve

It took every bit of his willpower not to kiss her. His whole body had gone rogue and for what? Because some pretty, spunky woman had been concerned over his welfare? If he'd allowed himself to become attached to every woman who faked caring about him, he'd have been married and divorced half a dozen times by now.

Zane shot her a look once more. She appeared frozen in place. Her brows were drawn together, and she stared at a spot on the ground. He had to hand it to her: she was smart. It hadn't taken much for him to remind her that neither one of them wanted to get tied up in some relationship that wouldn't last.

If his own mother didn't want to stay for him, what made him think someone like Ansley would?

But none of that mattered at the moment. They were stranded, and someone should have come looking for them by now. There was only one option he could see, and Ansley had already shot it down. He'd have to carry her back.

She shivered beside him, setting his decision in stone. "I know you don't like it, but we can't stay out here. We have to at least make it to the fork. No one is going to come looking for us out here."

Ansley frowned but didn't shift her focus toward him. Her eyes had clouded over with something he couldn't decipher.

Zane rotated his ankle and found the pain from before already easing up a little. It had been sore but not enough to stop him—slow him down, maybe, but not stop him. He climbed to his feet and held out his hand toward Ansley. "Come on, I'll give you a piggyback."

Her body remained stiff and unmoving. She wouldn't look at him.

"You okay?"

Still nothing except another shiver.

"Come on, Ansley. We have to start moving. You're cold and hurt. I'm not going to let you freeze out here." He leaned down and grasped her upper arm.

She yanked her arm away from him. "Don't touch me," she snapped. "We wouldn't be out here if you had been paying attention."

There it was, the reaction he'd been expecting all along. No one was perfect. Not even Ansley was able to put aside her selfishness for long. It didn't matter that she was right regarding his driving them up this path. They were in this predicament together, and they'd have to continue sticking together to get out of it. He let out a frustrated sigh and reached for her again, garnering another glare from her.

"I'm staying right here until they find us. It won't be long."

"You don't have any choice in the matter. Like I said, I'd rather deal with your wrath than Kate's." This time, he didn't just reach for her arm to help her to her feet. He scooped her up and tossed her over his shoulder. His muscles groaned in protest, but the short burst of adrenaline that had occurred from getting her over his shoulder helped him power through.

Ansley yelped and commenced pounding her fists on his back. "Put me down."

"Not until we hit the fork in the path up ahead."

"You shouldn't be walking on your foot, let alone carrying me."

"Don't pretend you care about my well-being."

She stilled, the fight having gone out of her. Good. The line in the sand had been drawn. They knew their expectations for each other.

But then she had to go and open her mouth. "I don't care if you believe me, but I do care."

He snorted. People tended to show their true colors when they were stressed or hurt. She might have tricked him at first, but he'd seen through it. He'd been a fool to think she might be someone he could consider dating long term.

His boots sank into the snow with each step, and his breathing was becoming more labored. Flashes of their accident flickered in front of his eyes like stars. The sight of her crumpled body on the ground. The sound of her gasp when she'd been hurt. The way her gentle touch had sent a pleasant shiver through his body. Her bright eyes so full of worry.

Zane attempted to right his thoughts. He shouldn't be thinking such things. They came to the fork, and he gently put her down just as a wave of dizziness overcame him.

He stumbled.

Ansley cried out.

The sound of motorized vehicles grew closer.

Everything went dark.

Zane blinked as a searing white light flooded his vision. He groaned and rolled onto his side. His head pounded, and his chest ached as if someone had stood on it. The surface he was lying on was soft, warm. They weren't outside in the cold anymore.

His eyes flew open, and he sat bolt upright.

"Shh. It's okay. We're back."

He whirled around to find Ansley's concerned blue eyes on him. Her nose was a little pink, as were her cheeks. He must not have been out for very long.

She didn't wait for him to even ask what had

happened. "Either you had a panic attack or you were suffering from shock. I told you not to strain yourself." She'd pulled his hand into her own. Neither one of them was wearing gloves now, and her skin was soft and warm against his.

Zane glanced around the room. It looked as if they were in some sort of nurse's office. He was on a cot with cushions. His coat was on a chair in the corner beside his boots. His focus shifted to his feet, and Ansley spoke up again.

"I told them you might have an injured ankle like me. Luckily, they don't think you'll have any issue putting weight on it."

He looked down to where her hand still held his. Then his gaze bounced up to meet hers.

She removed her hand from his grasp and fiddled with the hair resting over her shoulder. "Liam just stepped out to get some hot chocolate. He'll be right back."

"You stayed with me?" His voice was as hoarse as if he'd been passed out for days instead of less than an hour.

Her features pinched together in an adorable crease. "Of course I stayed. I wasn't going to let you wake up alone." Her hands dropped, and she looked away. "I owe you an apology."

It was hard not to stare at her as if she'd grown an extra head. What did she have to apologize for? He'd been the one to run them off the road. He'd been solely responsible for the predicament they'd found themselves in.

Still not meeting his gaze, she continued. "If you hadn't scooped me up and taken me to the end of the trail, there's no telling how long we would have been out there. Thanks to you, we were found." Ansley lifted her eyes to meet his. "I shouldn't have gotten mad at you—or made things harder." A pretty blush covered her whole face as she worried her lower lip. "I just wanted to make sure to apologize before I head up to bed."

She moved to stand, and his hand shot out to reach for hers. Ansley paused, that crease appearing between her brows again as she dragged her gaze to meet his.

A thousand thoughts raced through his mind as it argued and battled with the emotions in his heart. Was it possible he yearned for something more—not with just anyone but with Ansley? He hadn't expected to pass out. It *could* have been shock. But something told him the panic-attack theory was closer to being accurate.

That accident could have been so much worse. And he had nearly lost any chance he might have had with the woman in front of him.

"Zane?" she whispered. "Do you need me to get a nurse?"

He shook his head.

Spit it out. Just do it. You can ask her out. What are you waiting for? What's the worst that could happen?

She could say no.

Zane forced a smile. "Ansley?"

"Yeah?"

"I—"

"You're up. That's great." Liam entered the room, holding two cups with steam rising from the tops, and Ansley pulled her hand from Zane's grasp. Liam offered a cup to Ansley then held up the other. "You want one?"

Zane could have punched his cousin in the nose at that moment. He shook his head then met Ansley's gaze. "I'm glad you're all right."

Her smile was small, almost imperceptible. She nodded then slipped from the room.

Chapter Thirteen

The butterflies in Ansley's chest fluttered angrily. How dumb was that? She shouldn't have stuck around long enough for him to wake up. It had seemed like a good idea to begin with. She hadn't wanted him to wake up alone. And watching him rest so peacefully had introduced several other thoughts into the equation.

Zane was attractive. Boy, was he attractive. For all intents and purposes, he was exactly what she liked in a guy. He was tall with a dark complexion, and someone could drown in those eyes of his.

Ansley shook her head firmly. Zane was not an option. And she didn't even *want* a long-term relationship with him—or with anyone for that matter. She'd made that clear to everyone who bothered to listen.

Relationships never worked out. Not most of them, anyway. The divorce statistics in this country had continued to grow since before her own parents' divorce, and there was nothing anyone could do about it. No one was perfect enough. Those who stayed in relationships longer than a few years were the lucky few.

And yet...

No. Zane wasn't going to be the exception. He was just like she was. Neither of them was interested in the messiness that was marriage.

So why was she suddenly so disappointed with this entire situation?

No, not disappointed. Angry.

Ansley felt the indignation twist and coil in her stomach, filling every part of her. How dare he be sweet toward her? Didn't he know what that kind of behavior could do to a girl? Zane had her entertaining the idea of something more.

She was a fool. So was he for that matter. But she wasn't going to let him get to her anymore.

Ansley woke suddenly. Wait - it couldn't be morning already. She shot a look toward Kate, who was snoring soundly. Whatever had woken her from her sleep hadn't been as big as she'd originally thought. She lowered herself back into her covers and lay there, staring at the ceiling, wide awake.

A light tapping against the hotel room door sounded,

and she twisted her head in that direction. Her eyes narrowed. Had she imagined it?

Again, the distinct tick, tick, tick on her door echoed toward her.

Ansley sat up and glanced once more at Kate now that her eyes had adjusted to the darkness. Her roommate didn't seem disturbed in the slightest. Carefully, she crawled out of her bed and retrieved a robe to ward off the cold. Her feet landed softly on the plush carpet. There was no peephole in the door through which to check who might be visiting them so late, and she nearly scurried back to the warm confines of her bed. But another soft knock changed her mind. Whoever it was wouldn't be giving up so easily. She pulled aside the latch that locked the door and winced as it creaked with the effort.

One more look over her shoulder confirmed that Kate was a heavier sleeper than Ansley had given her credit for. Ansley pulled open the door and gasped. Zane had a hand resting on either side of the doorway. He lifted his head when the door made the sound, and his gray eyes bored into hers.

"Zane," she breathed, "what are you doing here?" Ansley shot one more look at Kate then tightened the belt of her robe. "It's the middle of the night," she hissed.

He worked his jaw. Straightening, he allowed his arms to drop to his sides. "I wanted to finish our conversation from earlier."

Brows furrowing, Ansley frowned at him. "What conversation?"

His breathing had grown more ragged. "When I woke up...and you were there."

She shook her head. "Zane, I don't think—"

"Why not?" he blurted.

"Pardon?"

"Why *shouldn't* we? I assume you're referring to something starting between us. Why dismiss the possibility so quickly?"

Ansley bit back a bark of laughter. "Are you serious? Look at who you're talking to. And *you*. You of all people would know why something between us would be a serious mistake."

The pain that flickered across his face was almost enough to make her retract her statement. Almost.

She heaved a sigh. "Think about it. If we even *entertained* a relationship, we would never hear the end of it from Liam and Kate. Then there's you, the glorified bachelor who won't give women more than two chances to change your mind."

"Well, that's hardly fair."

"And I don't believe marriage lasts. The evidence is stacked against—"

He held up both hands. "Whoa. Who said anything about marriage?"

Her face burned. In truth, Zane hadn't mentioned anything about a serious relationship. She scowled at him, folding her arms. "I'm not going to be a notch on your bedpost, Zane. I can understand your desire to have this two-date rule, but I don't respect it."

His scowl matched hers. "What about you? Don't you have a certain time frame in which you will break it off?"

She scoffed. "That's totally different. And it's not a set *time frame*. I end things when the relationship runs its course." Her voice rose, and she stiffened when she heard Kate moan.

He dragged his hand down his face. "Look, I didn't come here to fight."

"Then what did you come here for?" she snapped. "Because it sure looks like you're doing exactly what you *didn't* want to do."

Zane reached for her hand and pulled her into the hallway. She let out a gasp and stared up at him as the door shut behind her. He stared intently at their clasped hands. "Because you are the first person who has made me want to reconsider my two-date rule." He lifted his solemn eyes to meet hers, and their gray depths stirred a chill that raced through her, leaving her breathless. "I think I'm developing feelings for you."

Her mouth dropped open.

He chuckled and ran his free hand through his hair. Shaking his head, he traced his thumb over her knuckles. "I can't explain it other than to say that while we were on that mountain, I realized something."

The fluttering within her returned with a vengeance. She seemed unable to move, caught in the snare of his gaze. Her throat tightened, and she wasn't sure if she was feeling lightheaded from this conversation or from their accident earlier.

He reached for her other hand so he held both of them. "I realized that there is something about you that I'm totally and utterly drawn to. And when I found you crumpled in the snow, I'd never experienced being that terrified in all of my life." Zane moved even closer to her, and his voice lowered until it was just above a husky whisper. "There's something telling me if I don't take a chance..."

Ansley blinked. What did he want her to say? He couldn't just stop with that. What was he asking of her?

"Please tell me you feel it too," he murmured.

Chapter Fourteen

Zane searched Ansley's eyes for something—*anything*—that would confirm that he wasn't alone in these feelings. After the medic had cleared him to head to bed, he had not been able to relax. Every nerve ending was alive, on fire almost. The only thought that continued to run marathons in his head was of Ansley and the way she'd looked when he came to.

But as she stood before him as if he'd just turned her to stone with his confession, he felt even more alone than he had while waiting for her to open this dang door.

"Say something," he pleaded.

This wasn't like him. Standing in front of a girl, begging her to accept his offering, was foreign to him. How many times had he been on the other side of things? Countless. She could turn him down in this very moment, and he'd probably deserve it.

Ansley's gaze dipped to where he held her hands

tightly then drifted up to meet his. "Did you hit your head?"

"What?"

"That's the only reason I can think of as to why you would drag me out of my room and ask me to... what? Date you?"

"Ansley—"

She attempted to tug her hands free, but he wouldn't let her. "Because if you didn't hit your head, then you must be trying to prank me. Did Liam put you up to this?"

"*Ansley*—" The desperation of his voice was hard for him to swallow. He forced out a chuckle. "I didn't hit my head. I'm—putting myself out there. I... I like you."

"Why?"

His head reared back. "What kind of question is that?"

She shrugged. "What makes me so different?"

"Boy, you're not making this easy, are you?"

For the first time since she'd come out, he could sense a hint of a smile on her lips. "*Never*," she whispered.

Zane tipped his head, studying her features. "I could blame your beauty. I could say that your blond hair practically glows golden whenever you pass by a lit garland or tree. I could say that your blue eyes put the snow and ice outside to shame. But I won't."

"You won't?" Her lips twitched.

He shook his head, stepping close enough that he could drop her hands and move his hold to her waist. He dipped his face toward her so he could whisper near her ear. "No. Because it's more than that."

Her breath hitched, and her whole body seemed to stiffen at their closeness. "It is?" she whispered so softly he nearly didn't hear it.

"It's in the way you notice every single detail. The way you don't back down when you come up against a challenge. The way your eyes flash when you're giving someone a warning. But it's also in the way you so obviously care about your friends and in the way your concern overflows, even for someone you practically despise."

"I don't *despise* you," she mumbled.

"Don't you?" His warm breath filled the space between them, and she shivered within his arms. He pulled back just far enough to meet her eyes. The bright-blue color that he loved had darkened somewhat, filled with a desire he recognized. His gaze bounced momentarily to her lips. He could kiss her right now, capture her against himself. His chest tightened as his stomach swirled and heated.

It was almost imperceptible, but she leaned slightly toward him. Her chin tilted, and her lashes fluttered. She did want this just as he did. But there was a problem with that. He had done it wrong his whole life. If he wanted this to work, something had to change.

Zane released her, causing her to lose her balance. He reached out to steady her but kept her at arm's length. Ansley blinked rapidly and sucked in a deep breath before releasing it through pursed lips. Confusion clouded her vision. She moistened her lips, which only intensified the urge to gather her in his arms and kiss her as if it would be their last.

Instead, he clenched his hands at his sides, digging his fingernails into his palms. The bite centered him. Ansley hadn't answered him. She hadn't completely shot him down, either. That meant he had a chance.

The door beside them clicked, and they both jumped. Kate opened the door and poked her head out. "Ansley? Zane? What are you doing? It's the middle of the night."

Ansley darted for the door and held it open, blushing. "I hope we didn't wake you. We were just discussing wedding preparations." She shot Zane a look before smiling at Kate. "I'll be right in."

Kate's sleepy, confused stare bounced from her friend to Zane and back. "Okay."

Once she'd disappeared, Ansley let out a soft laugh. She clapped a hand over her mouth then grew serious. She lowered her hand and whispered, "You're crazy, you know that?"

He offered her a half smile. "I hear that happens when you like someone."

Ansley rolled her eyes.

Before she could make a comment about his feelings being ridiculous, he cut her off. "You don't have to say anything right now. But just think about it." He gave her a short nod and strode down the hall toward his own room. He could feel her eyes follow him until he turned a corner.

The second he was out of sight, he stopped and placed his palm against the wall. The pounding in his chest was causing a return of his lightheadedness. If he wasn't careful, he might pass out again. Luckily, the pain in his ankle had subsided to be more of an inconvenience than anything else. It was the way Ansley affected him that was causing his body to go haywire.

And it wasn't exactly unpleasant.

A smile spread across his face. It was tempting to turn on his heel and head right back to her door and steal that sensual kiss he'd nearly taken. But he'd be patient. It'd be hard, but something told him it would be worth the effort.

Zane pushed away from the wall and hurried back to his room. Once he'd snuck inside, he collapsed on the bed, laced his hands behind his head, and stared up at the ceiling. He'd snuck out to her room because he couldn't sleep. All he'd wanted was to let her know of his new feelings and see if there was any possibility she could feel the same.

It turned out that after seeing her, he was even more restless than before. But this time, he didn't mind so much. Any amount of sleep lost might just be worth it.

Chapter Fifteen

Most of the guests would arrive by this evening, and Ansley was nothing if not a good hostess. She spent most of the morning putting together little thank-you goodie bags for everyone. The gold paper bags were small, only large enough to hold two personal bottles of champagne, an itinerary, and a few candies. She tied each one with a red-and-green ribbon while listening to various Christmas songs play over the speaker in a conference room just down the hall from a large ballroom.

The task was mind numbing, which only created more problems. Every time her thoughts wandered, Zane filled them. His gray eyes and teasing smile gave her goose bumps, and her gaze darted to the doorway whenever anyone walked past.

He hadn't bothered to find her yet today, which offered both a semblance of relief and a great deal of anxiety. When he inevitably showed his face, what was she going to say? All night long, she had contemplated how things would progress if she just let go and risked being wrong.

It wasn't that she wanted to be right. Everything she'd told him about marriage and long-term relationships, she fully believed.

But there was something about Zane that made her want to be wrong. More than she'd ever wanted anything.

She pulled the green-and-red ribbon tight, connecting the two handles on top of a bag, and folded it into a pretty bow.

"You're pretty good at that."

Ansley jumped, a small squeak escaping her throat. Her gaze shot up to find Zane standing in the doorway as only he could. His arms were folded, and one foot crossed over his ankle as he leaned against the doorjamb.

His eyes swept over her face then her project then her face again. Zane propelled himself into the room and pulled out a chair.

Her eyes widened as she watched him grab two champagne bottles and a handful of candy and place them in the bag. He met her gaze and winked before he yanked a length of ribbon from the table and deftly matched what she'd just done. "But maybe I could give you a run for your money."

She made a face. "Cute," she muttered.

He chuckled and gathered the supplies for another one. "What are these for?"

Ignoring the fact that his presence seemed to make the room seem all that more small, she commenced putting together another one. "They're for the guests. We can't exactly have them come all this way and not thank them." She smiled as she looped the ribbon around her fingers and tightened the bow.

They worked in silence for a few moments, and every so often, she caught him staring at her. Finally, she sat back in her office chair and folded her arms. "What?"

Zane lifted one brow. "Really?"

She swallowed and forced her gaze to remain steady. She couldn't let him see that she wasn't just as brave as she'd always been, though the thought of succumbing to his ideas made her knees go weak without any additional help from him.

He stood and placed his hands on the table. "You can't honestly suggest that you don't know why I'm here —why I'm making goo-goo eyes at you. Or why I'd rather spend my morning putting together little gift bags for guests I couldn't care less about." He straightened and slowly made his way around the table, stalking her like the prey she'd allowed herself to become.

Ansley scooted her chair away from him, and her hands flew to the armrests as if that was enough to steady her racing heart. "I know why you're here."

His steps slowed, and he cocked his head. "Okay, so

why don't you save us both the trouble and admit you're intrigued."

"It was never a lack of intrigue, Zane." Her voice trembled when his name tumbled from her lips. She gave a sharp shake of her head. There was no way she'd let him get the upper hand in this conversation. "It's always been about time."

The way his brows wrinkled and his mouth twisted into a strange sort of smile made her stomach do a somersault. "Time? What on earth does that mean?" He took another step toward her.

Ansley's hands tightened on the armrests. "You know exactly what I mean. When you scope out a girl you're willing to take on those two dates, you're not going to waste your time on women who won't abide by that two-date rule. You can't tell me that you don't have the ability to decide in a moment. You probably had me figured out the second we met."

His smile widened further. "Am I correct in assuming you think you have me all figured out as well?"

She lifted a shoulder.

"Okay. I'll bite. Tell me, Ansley. Am I worth your *time*?" His voice had dropped to a husky timbre, and he was now close enough he'd managed to place his hands over hers on the armrests. His face was inches from hers, his warm breath caressing her cheek and causing chills to race down her spine.

Her mouth went dry, and her gaze dipped to his lips. The sly smile he wore was exactly the kind she assumed he'd use when he flirted with women he wanted to take out on dates. That smile was the only thing that held her back. If he was treating her the way he treated all those other women, then what made her so different?

Zane's thumb traced over the back of her hand, and he whispered, "I can tell what you're thinking."

"There's no way you would know something like that," she huffed, though her voice sounded less sure than she'd intended.

"You're wondering if I'm going to just end things like I usually do when everything goes back to normal and we head home."

He wasn't far off. "Well, are you?"

Zane studied her for several moments. "I don't know the future, Ansley. All I know is that I want to try something different. Do you know the definition of insanity?"

"It's doing the same thing—"

"Over and over and expecting a different outcome. Maybe I've finally realized that I don't want the same thing anymore." His eyes drilled into hers, making every hair on her arms stand on end. She could smell his cologne, and it only caused more disruption in her chest. Before she could offer him a retort, he cut her off. "Maybe I've realized I want you."

Chapter Sixteen

Zane didn't know what more he could do to win her over. Ansley was a hard nut to crack. The only problem he had was time—and not the same kind of time that she'd mentioned.

The fact that Ansley had mentioned that she wasn't sure about starting a relationship because it wouldn't be worth her time had stung like a slap in the face. But at the same time, she was right. He couldn't deny it.

Yes, he did scope out the women he wanted to date. There were signs he had learned to notice a long time ago. There were clingy women and those who believed in love at first sight. Those were the ones he had to stay far, far away from.

There were women like Ansley who didn't want anything more than something short and fun. And normally, he wouldn't have even bothered, because she'd made it far too hard for him. There was just one problem.

He couldn't stop thinking about her. There would be no shaking her from his mind. And from the looks of it, she wasn't convinced.

In one swift movement, he grasped her hands and pulled her to a standing position against his chest. One of his hands wrapped around her waist, and the other grasped her right hand. He swayed with, her and she let out a laugh.

"You're not seriously dancing with me, are you?"

"The way I see it, there's no risk for you. Let me woo you throughout the week, and when the wedding is over, then you decide. What do you say?" He dipped her, and she laughed again. "Will you be my wedding date?"

Slowly, he pulled her back up. Their swaying stopped, and her features sobered. Ansley's gaze darted to the table. "I have so much to do. I won't be much fun."

"I can help. I don't mind."

Her eyes darted to meet his. "You're kidding."

"I assure you, I'm very serious." He released her, and she took only a small step back—just enough that they were no longer touching.

The corner of her mouth lifted. "How can I resist such a proposition?"

He hooked his finger under her chin and brought his face closer to hers, not missing the sharp intake of breath. Her chest rose and fell, and a pretty flush covered her skin. The desire to kiss her overwhelmed him as her eyes fluttered closed.

She let out a soft exhale just as he brushed his lips against hers. It was brief and tentative, nothing like the kisses he shared with his conquests. But Ansley deserved something different. She deserved more, and he was going to be the one to give it to her.

In that moment, time slowed to a crawl. He could have seen a hummingbird's wings flap had one miraculously flitted by. Ansley's kiss was sweet and gentle—something that only made his pulse race faster for some reason. A kiss as chaste as this one shouldn't affect him the way it was. It was nothing more than a peck, but in that brief moment, he could see more. He could see a future with this woman.

It was the strangest thing, but at the same time, it was perfectly believable. Ansley was meant for him, and it had just taken these last few days for him to realize it.

Zane pulled back and smiled at her. His heart pounded, and the ache of wanting something more wouldn't abate. He withdrew and let out a shuddering breath. "So..."

"Yeah..." she agreed.

He chuckled and rubbed the back of his neck. He could pull her into his arms right then and there and ravish her until she had nothing left to give. But he wouldn't.

The right way. That was how this would go. She

needed to trust him. He gestured toward the table. "What do you need help with?"

Her focus swept over the table, and she pressed her lips into a thin line. "I only have a few more to make, and then we're going to take them to the front desk and see if the hospitality department will let us into the rooms of our guests."

"Wouldn't delivering them be the hospitality department's job?"

She clicked her tongue and shook her head. "Shame. And here I was beginning to think you really were getting to know me."

He slapped his hand to his forehead in a mock sign that he'd forgotten something. "Right. You and all your details." He moved to the table and placed a few of the newly crafted bags in a box with several others. "Well, then. Let's get to work so we can deliver these bad boys."

Ansley didn't move right away. Her deep sapphire eyes remained trained on him, studying him as if she could slip into his mind and discover the secrets he kept there.

Zane shifted and let out another nervous laugh. "*What*?"

She didn't miss a beat. "Why do you want to help me? I suppose it would make sense if you were guaranteed to get something out of this, but as it stands, I guess I don't see how helping me does anything for you."

Her statement was more or less correct. He didn't have to help her at this point. She'd already agreed to be his wedding date. His eyes narrowed slightly, and his lips quirked into a smile. "If it means I get to spend some time with you, that's enough for me."

Ansley scoffed. "You can't expect me to believe that."

"Believe it, baby. I'm going to woo you, and you're going to like every second of it."

She laughed. And it wasn't one of those fake laughs.

His whole body warmed, and he beamed at her. "I love that sound—when you laugh."

He thought his comment would unnerve her, but her smile didn't disappear at all. "You know, if you keep flirting with me like that, you might not be able to get rid of me." Her light tone bordered on teasing, but that was exactly what he wanted.

Zane moved toward her once more. With as much seriousness as he could muster, he murmured, "Maybe that's been the plan all along." He tucked a strand of blond hair behind her ear then let his fingertips graze the soft skin along her jaw.

Her arms rose and rested just behind his neck. The desire that pooled in his stomach returned. He needed to be careful. Getting too close too fast wouldn't be wise for either of them. But as she leaned toward him, teasing him, he couldn't help himself. Her soft whisper caused fresh goose bumps to appear on his arms. "Do you really think it will be so easy?"

He swallowed. There were so many sides to Ansley. This view of her was no less exciting. He grinned widely. "Give me *some* credit. You seem to have forgotten that I was surrounded by girls growing up. I've picked up more than just how to decorate."

"Oh?"

Zane nodded. "After we finish all of this up, what would you say to going ice-skating? If your ankle isn't still tender and you're feeling up to it. I'm sure we could steal a few hours before the dinner that's planned tonight."

"I'd like that." Her hands trailed down his chest before she let them drop to her sides and moved back to the table.

There was only enough material for five more gift bags. Zane placed them all in the box, and together, they headed for the front desk.

He kept sneaking glances at her, and each time he did, he caught her doing the same. She'd smile, and her fingers would capture a strand of hair to twist around them. He shifted the box to one arm and reached out to hold her hand.

Ansley looked down to where their fingers laced together and met his eyes with another shy smile. "I can't believe we're doing this."

"Me neither." He chuckled, bringing her hand to his lips. "But I'm glad we are."

Chapter Seventeen

Ansley hurried to her room to change into warmer clothing before heading out to the ice-skating rink. Zane had turned out to be quite the surprise. She had pegged him all wrong. It would have been nice to figure this out sooner.

Who was she kidding? She hadn't been ready to fall for someone until a couple of hours ago. A small smile touched her lips as she slipped into her hotel room and leaned against the door. Her hands traced the cool metal, and she let out a little laugh. Was this what Kate had been talking about when she'd said she thought she was falling for Liam?

Chills coursed through her body, and she had to rub her arms to rid herself of them. This was definitely something she had never experienced before. It was utterly amazing, and she wanted it to go on forever.

Ansley bit her lower lip and shook her head. If this

was love, then she was willing to accept it with open arms. She moved through the room, exchanged her blouse for a sweater, and grabbed her coat and gloves.

All she needed was a hat and—

Her phone buzzed, skittering across the lacquered wood desk. The smile was still on her face as she hopped over the bed to get to it. Zane was probably getting impatient. But the caller ID wasn't Zane.

Her grin melted from her features, replaced with a frown and twinges of anxiety. Her mother usually only called to complain about one thing. She hesitated. If she ignored her mother's call, Cora would inevitably call back again and again until she'd said her piece.

Ansley closed her eyes briefly and snatched the phone before it went to voicemail. She forced a happy voice and plastered a smile on her face for good measure. "Hi, Mom."

"Oh, good. I hope I'm not interrupting anything for your friend's little wedding."

"Actually—"

"Okay, well, I won't keep you, but I needed your input on something."

"Mom, I don't have time to—"

"Your father," she said with an exaggerated groan. "He's claiming that I can't have you for New Year's Eve this year. Well, I told him that since you're out at that wedding for Christmas, I get to have you for the next holiday."

Ansley pinched the bridge of her nose. Her heart

pounded a little harder. This happened every time her mother called to complain about her father. Every. Single. Time. "Mom, as we discussed—"

"You'll call him and let him know that he's wrong, right, dear? It's only fair. He can't steal you away from me. You're a grown woman, and you can make your own decisions."

"Mom. As much as I'd love to continue this conversation, I have a date."

Her mother gasped. "A date? Like a *date* date? Oh, be careful, Ansley. Don't go falling for the first guy who pretends to care about you. Heaven knows I learned my mistake. Your father—"

"*Mom*!" Ansley sighed. "My relationship with Zane is still new, and I'm not sure where it's going to go. But if I need your advice, I'll be sure to ask for it."

Her mother remained quiet on the other end of the line. Great. Now the guilt would replace the anxiety, and the cycle would start all over. It was almost as if her mother's failed relationship was a warning, forever emblazoned in Ansley's mind as something that was inevitable. Being in a relationship with Zane was an impossibility.

"I'll call you on Christmas, Mom," she murmured quietly. "Love you."

"Love you too, sweetheart." The tone indicating that her mother had hung up beeped into the receiver.

Ansley stared at the phone in her hand and shook her head. The happy, airy feeling she'd had when she'd entered this hotel room was depleted. Her stomach roiled, and suddenly, she didn't feel like going ice-skating anymore.

Was her future really doomed like her mother's? She scowled at the phone and threw it onto the bed. Even if it was, that future wasn't written yet. She couldn't let one failed relationship drag her down. She had to remember that there was proof things did work out. Kate and Liam had one of the healthiest relationships she could think of. And if they thought that Zane was a good fit for her, she should believe she had a chance.

She snatched her coat from the chair and shoved her arms into the sleeves. If she let her mother get to her, she didn't have even a sliver of a chance with Zane. She'd just have to keep looking toward Kate for her inspiration.

Ansley hurried down the hall, forcing every dark thought from her mind, which proved to be a bigger chore than she'd expected. The weight on her shoulders, the uncertainty—all of it seemed to pull on her.

Everything would be fine. Zane was perfect for her. They were good together.

She rode the elevator down to the lobby, the encouraging words in her brain on repeat. When the elevator doors slid open, Zane was there. The smile on his face was enough to melt the ice rink outside. Her legs went numb, and her heart fluttered.

And yet her mother's words came back to her. *Don't go falling for the first guy who pretends to like you.* She grimaced. How well did she really know Zane? He had that silly rule on dating. What if he *was* manipulating her? Then the darkest thought of all washed over her, turning her cold from the inside out. This could all be some challenge he'd concocted for himself.

He wrapped his arms around her, and she shivered. There was no way to know, of course. Even as she glanced up at him and found him staring at her, she couldn't tell.

"Is everything okay?" His brows furrowed, and he slowed his steps. "Are you getting sick?"

"What? No, of course not. Why would you even ask that?" She hated the way her voice trembled.

Dang it, she'd gotten into her own head—let her mother's distrust in—and now she was sabotaging the first relationship she was actually excited about. She shook her head to rid herself of those debilitating thoughts and plastered a smile she didn't feel onto her face.

"I'm just a little tired. I'll be fine with some fresh air."

He didn't look convinced. Of course he wouldn't believe her. He had trust issues too. Maybe their match wasn't the most thought out. She dragged her feet as they headed for the entrance to the resort. She needed a minute to think.

They made it out into the crisp, cold air. More Christmas songs played loudly over the speakers outside, but she couldn't focus on the music.

A few yards away, frustrated voices drew the attention of those around them. Ansley's head swiveled around, and she spied Liam and Kate squaring off. Both of them looked absolutely flustered, red in the face, and about ready to storm off themselves.

This wasn't happening. It couldn't be. Kate and Liam had the perfect relationship. Their wedding was in a couple days. They couldn't be arguing right now. Shouldn't they be in a state of nearly wedded bliss?

Her breaths came out faster and faster. A pounding started in her head, and Ansley closed her eyes. It was as if she was in the middle of a concrete room, and the walls were closing in on her. No matter how strong she was, she couldn't push them back.

"I made a mistake," she blurted.

Zane moved between her and their friends, blocking them from view. "Ansley?"

She met his gaze for just one second then shook her head. "I'm sorry. I can't." She spun on her heel and charged inside the resort. She was an idiot for thinking that she could have anything more than failed relationship after failed relationship. She wasn't special no matter how much she wished she was.

Chapter Eighteen

Zane watched Ansley disappear inside the building, gaping after her. What had that been about? Confusion twisted like a rogue tornado in his head. Had he said something wrong? *Done* something wrong?

He glanced over his shoulder, where Liam and Kate's argument seemed to be at a standstill. What could possibly be so upsetting that they had to air their dirty laundry in front of an audience? His jaw tightened, and he shook his head. He'd deal with them later. Right now, Ansley was clearly going through something.

His whole body was on edge, tingling with an irritating electricity. He brushed past a few couples who had exited the building and charged in the direction Ansley had gone. It was one thing to let her run away because she wanted a little space and something entirely different for her to abandon him after making some cryptic comments.

Zane slowed his steps. What if she'd run because she didn't want Kate to see them together? She'd mentioned that she didn't want their friends to tease her about this setup. She had agreed to give their little relationship a trial run, but deep down, he'd hoped that had meant she was all in. Maybe he was a fool. He shouldn't have assumed anything. Ansley was a firecracker who didn't trust easily. That was the first thing he'd learned about her.

He ran a hand through his ragged hair as he got to the elevator. A couple was waiting for it, and the button was already lit to go up. He shifted his weight from one foot to the other and stared at the numbers at the top of the elevator. The longer this took, the less likely he'd be able to convince Ansley that everything was going to be fine.

Visions of her pale face and the pain in her eyes flooded his mind. Something had happened to her between the time he'd left her to get warmer clothes and the time she had arrived in the lobby. He'd just have to make her tell him so he could fix it.

If he could fix it.

Zane swallowed the unease that came up his throat like heartburn at that thought. He wasn't known for repairing a broken relationship once one of them had ended it. He might not even be very good at it.

The doors opened, and he shot inside. The couple

who'd been waiting stepped in after him, the love in their gazes almost too much to handle. He averted his gaze when they leaned in close and kissed.

His insides twisted with pain as if they already knew what the outcome of this conversation would be. He wasn't going to be able to fight fate. Maybe it was karma. He'd hurt too many women with his stupid dating rules, and now that he'd finally found one he wanted more than anything, she'd be ripped right out of his hands.

The elevator doors slid open, and he trudged out onto Ansley's floor. He could stop right here in the hallway and pretend that nothing had happened. She hadn't broken up with him. She was just going through something, and when she'd had a minute to breathe, she'd come find him and tell him as much.

Even as he thought the words, he found himself staring at her door like he had that night he'd come to talk to her when he couldn't sleep. Zane lifted his hand, letting his fist hover a few inches from the door.

He should leave.

She needed space, right?

If he cornered her now, that would only lead to disappointment.

No. That was the fear talking. For the first time in his life, he actually wanted a relationship with someone. Just because his mother had walked out on his father didn't mean he was destined for the same thing. Ansley was good and kind, and she'd make a wonderful mother. She didn't have a bad bone in her body, and he would die before letting his fear strangle what happiness he still had available to him.

He rapped firmly on the door.

No answer.

She had to be in there. Running anywhere else would be unwise. There were too many guests who could walk in on her in the conference rooms or the ballroom.

Zane knocked again, more loudly this time. "*Ansley.*" His voice was gruffer than he'd meant it to be. He blamed the sniveling inner coward he'd forced himself to dispose of. "Ansley, I know you're in there, and I'm not going anywhere until we talk."

"Go away, Zane."

His jaw tightened, and a muscle in his cheek right below his right eye twitched. "Did you not hear me? I said I'm not going anywhere until you talk to me."

"I don't want to talk, Zane. I apologize for misleading you. Can't that be enough?" Her voice was closer this time, right on the other side of the door.

Zane pressed his palm against the door, and his voice softened. "I don't know what you're going through, but I want to help. Let me help you."

"There's nothing you can do, Zane. I was an idiot. I thought—" It was clear she'd cut herself off when he strained to hear the rest of her sentence but got nothing.

"What did you think?" His voice broke when he heard the sadness in hers. If he could have, he would have burst through the door so he could wrap his arms around her and tell her everything would be okay.

"I thought that things could be different. But I was wrong."

Zane rested his forehead against the door and squeezed his eyes shut, letting the cold surface ease the pounding there. "Why can't they be different? Help me understand."

"They just can't. I'm not going to spend the rest of my evening trying to explain to you what I know to be true when you'll just fight me on it."

He rubbed his forehead back and forth against the door as he shook his head and let out a heavy breath. It was getting harder to keep his cool when she wasn't giving him anything to work with. His next words came out through gritted teeth. "If you already know I'm going to fight you, then maybe you already know that you're wrong, and you just don't want to accept it."

"Just—go away, Zane. Please. I don't want to see you right now."

"Why? Because you'll change your mind?" His voice rose a decibel, and he stepped back to glower at the door. "If that's the case, then I can make you a promise. The only person standing in your way is you. And if you can't see that, then maybe you're right. Neither one of us deserves to be happy."

Zane stomped down the hallway, his fists at his sides. He'd gotten off lucky. Already, he could feel his temperature rising and the fury pooling in his veins.

A snide little voice in his head muttered, *I told you so.*

Chapter Nineteen

Ainsley took in a deep breath and let it out through pursed lips. Sitting on the floor with her back against the door, she probably looked more pathetic than she felt—which was a pretty big feat. She dragged her fingers beneath her eyes then pressed her hands to her cheeks. Her shaky breathing wasn't getting any better, and her whole body trembled.

She shook out her hands. This was not a normal reaction. She'd dated several people over the years. Zane was just another guy she could have fun with and move on from, right? Sure, he sounded upset, but he'd realize that she was right.

Neither one of them had wanted this from the very beginning. It was this resort. It had to be. Everyone here seemed to fall in love—or think they were falling in love. She and Zane had only gotten swept up in the thrill of it all.

Once he cooled off, she'd calmly explain to him that this was for the best. He was a rational guy. It would be fine.

Ansley dragged herself from the floor and wandered across the room toward her bed. She perched on the edge and stared at the wall, not really feeling that she could do anything else. All of her energy had been zapped as the realization of everything came crashing down on her.

She didn't know what Kate and Liam were arguing about, but it wasn't good. They might get over it. They could still follow through with the wedding. Then, in five or so years, they'd end up just like her parents.

That sick, twisty feeling in her stomach grew more insistent. She threw herself back on her bed and curled up on her side, urging the nausea to leave. If breaking up had been the right thing to do, then why was she still feeling as if her whole world hung in the balance?

Fresh air. That was what she needed.

But how was she going to get out there without being caught? Zane could be lurking on any floor or waiting by any doorway.

Ansley let out a groan. What had she turned into? She wasn't some wimpy little girl, afraid of seeing the guy she'd just broken up with. She was a strong, powerful, confident woman, and she didn't have to explain herself to anyone.

She sat upright and looked around the room for the coat she'd flung aside when she'd returned to her room in the first place. It was sprawled on the floor near the bathroom entrance. She jumped from the bed and hurried over to it. Swiping it from the floor, she wasted no time putting it on and taking off into the hall.

Her head pounded, and her heart beat with a ferocity that she hadn't experienced since her first kiss with Zane. Even though she wasn't worried about seeing him, that didn't mean she wanted to be stopped on her way outside. Taking the stairs was a better option than running into him on the elevator—less chance of being confined to a small space with him.

She cut down a hallway toward the stairwell and slipped inside. Each step away from her hotel room seemed to bring even more clarity to the situation. There was a reason she wanted to stay single for the time being. Yes, she based all of her decisions on the relationships she'd observed between other people. But she'd also been content—happy even—most of the time.

Not everyone needed a significant other to feel completed. And she fell into that category.

There was another twinge in her stomach, as if it disagreed with her mind's sentiment. Well, that was too bad. Logic had to win this argument for the sake of her sanity. She couldn't spend the rest of her life worrying about when the other shoe would drop. And she refused to be a victim.

Ansley burst into the bright white of the cold afternoon. She blinked and held up her hand to shade her eyes. Dang it, she'd forgotten her sunglasses. It probably wouldn't be wise to go ice-skating. But there were trails she could hike. And there was less possibility of running into anyone she'd rather not see.

Up, up, up the trail she continued hiking.

She'd done the right thing. There were no other options. Her mother had made it clear that even people who were in love could fall out of love. Kate had proven that even new love could easily fall to pieces. Maybe Ansley and Zane were just too different.

But people got into arguments all the time. Kate wouldn't want to marry someone who was just like her. That would be boring. That was why her and Liam's public argument had burned through Ansley so deeply. Kate was the most level-headed person she knew.

Ansley's steps slowed as the realization flooded her thoughts. Just because they were arguing didn't mean they wouldn't work it out. If anyone could figure out how to come to a compromise, it was Kate.

Her thoughts shifted to Liam and every *single* thing he'd done to win Kate back after the fiasco at the resort last year. He knew how to fight for what he wanted. He wouldn't just let one argument destroy their relationship. And even if he considered doing as much, there was no way Kate would let that happen.

Heck, there was no way *she'd* let that happen. What was a maid of honor supposed to do if not smooth the rough edges of the days leading up to the wedding?

Shoot!

She turned around and stared down the mountain at the resort, which had shrunk in size. Something sharp stabbed through her chest right where her heart rested beneath her ribcage. She sucked in a sharp breath and held her hand there.

An overreaction.

She had probably sounded like an absolutely crazy person to Zane. It was no wonder he'd stormed off. He'd pleaded with her—*begged* her to talk to him. He'd been the logical one, and she'd only given in to the fears she'd been harboring since her parents had split up.

Her legs trembled and gave out beneath her as she slumped to the ground in the snow. What if she'd messed up everything so badly that she couldn't get him back? What could she do to make it up to him?

A flurry of thoughts flooded her head, most of them utterly ridiculous. There was no grand gesture she could offer that would make him feel better after she'd yelled at him. She placed her head in her hands, feeling the red-hot emotion overtake her again.

Like a movie playing in slow motion, every interaction she'd had with him flickered through her head. That time he'd literally caught her. The way he'd dragged her from their snowmobile crash to where they'd get found. His smile from across the room. The way he teased her. The late-night confessions. How he could make her laugh.

She'd made the biggest mistake of her life.

It felt as if she'd gone through the worst whiplash ever, going from pushing him away to wanting him back. Maybe she could plead temporary insanity.

She had to come up with something.

Chapter Twenty

Z ane stormed back to the elevator and punched at the button to take him down to the lobby. He didn't know what he was going to do, but he did know one thing. Whatever had triggered Ansley had had to do with seeing Liam and Kate.

He gritted his teeth so hard that by the time the elevator arrived in the lobby, his jaw ached. The march through the foyer and outside went faster than he'd counted on, and he still didn't have the words to express what he felt inside.

Liam and Kate were no longer arguing. Instead, they were sitting on a bench, talking. They still didn't look very happy, but at least they weren't making a spectacle of themselves.

Zane charged up to them, his boots crunching against the salted cement. He jabbed a finger at them. "*You.*"

Kate jumped, but Liam looked up at him almost lazily. "What do you want, Zane? We're kinda dealing with something."

"Yeah. No kidding."

They had the gall to appear more confused than ever. Zane groaned. "Do you guys even know what you just did?"

They exchanged looks.

He threw his hands into the air. "You two were arguing for all the world to see."

"So what?" Liam's frustrated voice did nothing to ease the tension Zane felt all over.

"Are you kidding me? People were watching. I don't know what was so important that the two of you had to fight like that the day before your wedding and in front of your guests!"

Finally, an expression he could expect from them. Chagrined, they glanced at one another then him before they shifted their focus elsewhere.

"He's right, Liam," Kate murmured. Her gaze cut to Zane again. "Did someone say something?"

"You bet someone said something." His chest heaved, and he pointed up at the resort building as if they all had x-ray vision. "Ansley just called the whole thing off."

Kate's brows pulled together, and she shot out of her seat. "What? I have to go talk to her."

Liam's hand reached for hers, pulling her back into a seated position beside him. "I don't think that's a good idea, Kate."

She glowered at him. "She's my *friend*, Liam."

"And I'm your *husband*."

"Not yet," she muttered.

Zane shook his head. "What is up with you two?" He threw his hands into the air and paced in front of them. "A few days ago, you couldn't have been more in love. What on earth happened?"

Liam appeared more guilty at that point.

Zane zeroed in on that, coming to a stop in front of him. "What did you *do*?" he hissed.

His cousin stiffened, his eyes wide. "Nothing."

Kate snorted.

Liam glanced at Kate then to his hands, which were now in his lap. "I guess we didn't realize that Kate's ex had been invited to the wedding by accident."

Zane's eyes widened, but he didn't say anything. This was a mess. Had that creep actually showed up? Suddenly, the animosity between the two of them made sense.

Liam took a deep breath and let it out slowly. "I got upset and said a few things I shouldn't have."

Kate huffed again, her arms folded. "You should have known I would never have invited him."

He raked a hand through his hair and glanced at her from the corner of his eye. "Yeah. I know. I'm sorry."

The last few words were mumbled so quietly, Zane wasn't sure he'd heard them right. But based on the way Kate seemed to relax, it appeared that was exactly what Liam had said.

Zane pressed his lips together in a thin line. "So what do you want to do about it?"

Liam lifted a shoulder. "I guess there's nothing we can do."

"Didn't the guy get married to someone else?" Zane shifted his weight from one foot to the other. If that guy had the gall to show up to this wedding, he had to be up to something.

"He's not with her anymore," Kate murmured quietly. "I think that's why Liam was so upset. He thought—"

"I might have implied that Kate had invited him to give him a chance to win her back." Liam's face flushed red.

"Are you an idiot? Seriously, I need to know. Because that has got to be the stupidest thing I have ever heard. That woman sitting beside you is madly in love with you, Liam. And you were willing to risk it all because you were *jealous*?"

Liam flinched.

Zane let out a sigh, pinching the bridge of his nose. "I guess love really does strange things to people. Like I asked before, what do you want to do? Do you want him gone? His invite rescinded? Whatever you want, I'll do it. I just need you guys to kiss and make up."

That was when Kate seemed to notice how his agitation seemed excessive. Her eyes narrowed, and she scooted closer to Liam to hold his hand. "You like Ansley," she whispered.

Zane rolled his eyes.

"No, I mean, *really* like her. Zane—are you in *love* with Ansley?"

He resumed his pacing, the ache in his chest worsening. They hadn't exactly admitted to feeling that intensely toward one another. Deep down, he'd continued to fight against thoughts of ineptitude. He didn't feel he was good enough for her. But at this moment, that didn't seem to matter as much.

His steps slowed then came to a stop, and he faced his friends. "Yes."

Kate and Liam exchanged knowing smiles.

"Shut up," Zane muttered.

Liam set a fake innocent gaze on him. "I didn't say a word."

"It doesn't matter anyway. She doesn't want anything to do with me. She said she was wrong and that she didn't have the time to explain it to me. The only thing that matters right now is fixing whatever mess I just walked in on and make sure we get you two down the aisle before anyone else who shouldn't be here shows up."

Kate leaned forward. "But don't you want to fight for her?" She glanced at Liam. "When you finally find real love, you have to fight for it. You can't just let it slip through your fingers."

"What would you have me do, Kate? I can't force that woman to love me back." His voice broke, and emotion tore from his throat. "We've barely been dating. I can't expect her to share those feelings for me yet."

"I think she already does."

He shook his head. "If she felt that way, she wouldn't have let whatever this was happen."

Kate stood, releasing Liam's hand before she grasped Zane's shoulders. "You don't know her like I do. She's gone through some pretty tough stuff—especially regarding her parents' divorce. If I had to guess, I'd say she is terrified that getting closer to you means she will inevitably end up like them."

Liam's brows furrowed. "Didn't you say once that her parents hate each other?"

"Oh, they despise each other. They use her all the time to manipulate each other even though they haven't been together for at least fifteen years." She gasped, and her hand flew to her mouth. "I bet that's what happened. She still takes turns spending time with her parents on the holidays. She's going to miss Christmas." Her gaze locked onto Zane's. "She got a call from one of her parents. That has to be it." She turned him around and pushed him toward the hotel. "You have to fight for her, Zane."

He whirled around to scowl at the two of them. "I tried that already. She wouldn't talk to me."

Kate shook her head. "You can't give up. I know it's not fair. But you have to prove to her that you're going to be around for the long haul. She needs to know you won't abandon her and that you love her."

"It can't be that easy."

Liam chuckled. "Oh, it's not. She might not even believe you. It could take months or years to repair the damage her parents did. The only thing you have to worry about is whether or not it's worth the effort and the risk."

There wasn't a question in his mind.

Ansley was worth it all.

Chapter Twenty-One

Ansley rushed through the hotel toward his room. That was the first place that came to mind when she thought about where he might have gone. They were on a mountain. Eventually, he'd have to come back there. If she needed to, she could wait outside his hotel room and beg him to forgive her.

The hallway was empty of guests. She spotted a maid's cart about halfway down, and it looked as if it was in front of his room. Ansley hurried toward the cart and made it to the room, completely out of breath, just as the maid exited Zane's room—her old one. If the maid was cleaning Zane's room, he probably wasn't inside. That meant she could wait there for him to return while she gathered her thoughts.

The maid jumped, offered a polite smile, then stepped out of the doorway. Luckily, she was trusting enough to believe this was Ansley's room.

Darting inside, Ansley let the door shut quietly behind her. The beds were made, and the place was tidy. For two guys staying in this room, it looked awfully neat. She moved through the room toward the bed she assumed was Zane's. He didn't have anything on the bedside table, but the suitcase that she'd found when she'd come into the room at the beginning of her stay was sitting there at the foot of the bed.

She settled onto the edge, her fingers tracing the comforter. When he came, she'd have to be ready for him to be reasonably upset with her.

Ansley cringed. She'd always hated when her parents fought. In fact, she had run and hidden during most of it. But this was different. She needed to fix it because she was solely responsible.

A sigh escaped her lips, and she lay back on the bed to stare at the ceiling. The designs blurred the longer she stared at them. Her head ached, her eyes burned, and the skin on her face felt tight and scratchy from her tears. All of this combined to cause a slight drowsiness.

Her hands clasped on her stomach, she scowled, blinking a few times to keep herself awake. Knots in her stomach twisted, becoming worse by the second. The longer she waited, the heavier her lids became and the more freely her thoughts drifted. Zane's features materialized in her mind. His concerned eyes when they were out in the snow. No one had ever looked at her like that before. That was probably the first moment she'd realized he was something different. She should have accepted it then. Now, it might be too late to fix the mess she'd made.

What she wouldn't have given to turn back time and deal with that phone call with her mother in a more mature way. She would have reminded her mother that pitting her against her father wasn't appropriate. They were both her parents, and she wanted to love each of them equally.

Then, witnessing the argument between Liam and Kate had just set everything spinning. It wasn't a good excuse. It wasn't an excuse at all. She wasn't Kate, and Liam wasn't Zane. They had their own way of dealing with things, and she couldn't compare her own relationship to anyone else's. Or rather, she shouldn't. Ansley groaned and shut her eyes tight against the embarrassment that threatened to overwhelm her. She was a nutcase, and Zane would be lucky to get as far away from her as he could.

But she didn't want that. Not anymore.

She wanted him. Tears sprang to her eyes. If she couldn't get him back, what would she do? Just the thought of starting over with someone else made her feel even sicker to her stomach than she already was.

Ansley curled up on her side, her hand between her face and the blanket as a single tear slipped from her eye. Zane was a good guy. He'd even tried helping her talk through this—at least, that was what it had felt like. He deserved much better, and she would be darned if she couldn't be that for him.

At some point, her sad thoughts melted and muddled with her good memories of Zane. Her body relaxed, and the pounding in her head seemed to dissipate. The ache eased, and the bed beneath her seemed to give her a warm, comforting hug. She floated and curled deeper into its softness as her mind got swallowed by darkness.

"Ansley," a male voice whispered from somewhere on the outskirts of the oblivion she found herself in. "Ansley, wake up."

She knew that voice. It was familiar, comforting. It was a voice she wanted to be closer to. It was one she just knew she could trust. Ansley wandered toward it.

"Ansley," he murmured again. Something soft touched her cheek, sending rippling chills throughout her whole body.

Her eyes fluttered open. She blinked a few times in the dim room before her focus landed on him.

Only the top of Zane's head was visible. The rest of him was hidden by the side of the bed. His eyes were red rimmed and full of pain. Or maybe she was seeing something reflected in him that she found inside herself.

A gasp tore from her throat, and she bolted upright. When had she fallen asleep? The last thing she could remember was closing her eyes against the headache that refused to go away. A sharp pain shot through her head, and she closed her eyes against the flashes that assaulted her. She'd sat up too fast, and the vertigo was messing with her more than she expected.

She placed a palm to her forehead and moaned. When would her head stop spinning? She needed to get her bearings and fast.

Something light and warm touched her knee. She jumped, and her eyes flew open just as Zane settled onto the edge of the bed beside her. The mattress groaned with the shift of weight. Without provocation, he reached for her free hand.

Ansley studied him as he laced his fingers through hers almost solemnly. He traced his finger along the back of her hand and didn't speak. The room was dark except for the light coming from a nearby lamp. How long had she been asleep?

Oh crap! What about Kate's brother? Had he come in here and seen her? This day was getting worse by the second. A large lump formed in her throat, stubborn and unwilling to be moved no matter how hard she swallowed.

"Zane," she rasped. "I'm—"

He shook his head sharply, and she snapped her mouth shut. He took a deep breath and let it out through pursed lips. This was it. He was going to tell her he'd had plenty of time to think things over, and he'd realized he had been wrong in choosing her.

Chapter Twenty-Two

Zane had to tread carefully. Based on what Kate had said about Ansley's parents, if he said even one thing that could trigger her, he'd lose her. Liam's words had been on repeat as he'd watched Ansley sleep.

She might not believe him.

She might not ever believe him, but if she did, it could take a long time.

Kate's brother had come back about an hour ago, and Zane had sent him away. It might not have been appropriate to stay in this room with Ansley, but he wasn't about to wake her from a nap she probably needed more than anyone else in this hotel. She'd been burning the candle at both ends and was visibly stressed.

Even as she sat beside him, fidgeting as if she was about to bolt, he had to fight the urge to tighten his hold on her. He wasn't about to let her escape before he said his piece. Heck, after watching her sleep for a couple hours, he wasn't so sure he'd let her go without getting a confirmation that he'd won her back.

Zane shot a look in her direction and offered her a feeble smile. "I need to talk to you about what happened today."

She nodded. That was good. At least she was open to a discussion now.

"Something bad occurred between the time we finished up those little deliveries and when we met in the lobby, didn't it?"

Another nod.

"Do you want to tell me about it?"

Ansley paled then looked away. She tugged on her hand but not hard enough to pull it free.

"It's fine if you don't. But I think this conversation is going to go a heck of a lot better if you do." He ducked his head, waiting for her to meet his gaze. "I talked to Kate."

Her eyes shot to meet his. "What did she say?"

"I think it would be better for you to tell me about what happened in your hotel room."

Ansley shifted again then let out a long sigh. "I don't know if it's that important."

Zane worked his jaw from side to side. "When you refused to talk to me earlier, I stormed down to confront Liam and Kate. I was *sure* that whatever you were dealing with had something to do with them." He rubbed the back of his neck and shook his head. "Now, I feel like that was only a small part. Like a spark that lit the flame."

Her lower lip trembled. "I'm really messed up, Zane. I have no idea why you even like me, let alone want to date me."

"I don't like you," he murmured.

She stiffened, and her face filled with color. "Is this because of our fight? I didn't mean—"

"I love you, Ansley."

"I—you—*what*?" Her mouth dropped open, and all the fight went out of her. For the first time since she'd woken up, he could tell he'd shocked her.

The corners of his mouth twitched. "I love you, Ansley. As much as I wish I could, I can't explain it."

"You're—you have to be joking. Did Kate put you up to this?"

His brows furrowed. "What? Why would you even ask that? Do you honestly think that Kate would pull that kind of stunt? No, of course not."

"Are you sure?"

Zane moved closer to her, grasping her other hand within his own. "I couldn't be more sure of anything in my life."

"But—" Her gaze flitted to different objects in his hotel room. "I thought for sure you would think that I'm more trouble than I'm worth."

He let out a laugh. "Oh, you are definitely trouble."

She gave him a sharp look, and he reached out to tuck a strand of blond hair behind her ear.

"But if there's something I've realized in the last twenty-four hours, it's that I wouldn't have it any other way."

Her features softened. "Really?"

His fingers traced down her jaw, and he grasped her chin with his finger and thumb. "Really."

A tear slipped down her cheek, and she brushed it away with the back of her hand.

"Can you at least tell me why I found you asleep on my bed like Goldilocks?"

She let out a sharp laugh and looked away.

"Because I spent about two hours waiting for you to open your door like a fool until Kate came back to your room and let me in to see for myself that you'd left."

Ansley's eyes widened, and she let out another laugh, softer this time, before she dropped her gaze to her lap. "I came to tell you—that I was sorry. I shouldn't have reacted that way. I'd just gotten off the phone with my mother, and then with Kate and Liam —it was just so overwhelming. I wasn't thinking clearly."

So Kate had hit the nail on the head. Ansley was dealing with a lot more than just anxiety over her friends' argument. She had to work through whatever it was her mother had said to her. At this point, she didn't want to talk about it.

He pressed his lips into a firm line. "I shouldn't have

taken off so quickly. I should have made you talk to me. I could have helped—"

She shook her head vehemently. "No, you couldn't have."

His brows creased.

Ansley swallowed hard and pinned him with a serious gaze. "I never wanted a serious relationship, Zane. If you recall, in the beginning, it was hard to convince me to even play along just for fun." She sucked in a shuddering breath and let it out through pursed lips. "I've only ever watched relationships fail. Over and over. With that being the only examples of what marriage could offer, I decided a long time ago that I didn't want that. Love didn't exist."

She was wrong. He loved her. But he couldn't say that—not right now. It would undermine the trust she was finally willing to offer him.

"When my parents divorced, they used me as this sort of leverage against each other."

His stomach roiled. What kind of parents could do something like that to their daughter? Despite what Kate and Liam had told him, he'd thought they had to be exaggerating. Unfortunately, Ansley was proving otherwise. It was surprising she'd turned out as well-adjusted as she was.

Then again, people could probably have said the same about him.

"Anyway, I think I'd just gotten into my head about the whole thing, and I know I need to work on that.

Only, I can't promise that I will get better all that quick."
She grimaced. "And there's this small part of me that
knows you deserve more. I can't ask you to hang around
to deal with all my baggage—"

"Why not?"

She blinked at him but didn't give him any answers.

"Answer the question, Ansley. Why can't you ask me
to 'deal' with you? Because from where I'm standing,
that's the only thing I want to do."

"You have to stop saying perfect little things like
that."

"I'm damaged too, Ansley."

More shock.

"My mother abandoned my father—and me. I'm in
constant fear that any woman I allow myself to get close
to will do the same."

Her hand flew to her mouth. "I'm so sorry, Zane."

He made a dismissive gesture. "I'm fully aware of my
issues on this matter. It's why I made that two-date rule.
But it doesn't mean I won't be triggered. I might even get
a little paranoid. So as far as I'm concerned, you and I
make quite a unique pair."

She chuckled. "Are you sure you want to risk that?
We could be as catastrophic as vinegar and baking soda."

"Not catastrophic, no."

"What, then?"

"Epic." His mouth pulled into a wide smile. "But
you have to promise me one thing."

She stared at him blankly.

"You have to love me too."

Ansley grinned. "Deal."

"That's not what I requested."

This time, she laughed. "*Okay*, I get it." Outwardly, her features grew serious, but he could see the humor resting just beneath the surface. "I love you too, Zane."

Chapter Twenty-Three

Ansley stood beneath the archway, holding a small bouquet of flowers. She shifted her weight from one foot to the other. Zane was late, and the pianist was sure to start playing the wedding march at any moment. A few feet behind her, Kate was probably dealing with her own anxieties.

She glanced over her shoulder toward her friend and tossed her a smile. Kate smiled brightly back. Maybe Kate wasn't so anxious after all. It was almost unbelievable the way some people could come back from arguments as if they'd never happened, although her own parents hadn't managed to figure that out.

Rising onto her toes, Ansley peered through the crowd. Where was Zane? Her heart rate increased as she swung around and nearly bumped into a young woman with a clipboard.

Her hair was dark and pulled into a knot at the nape

of her neck. She couldn't have been more than twenty-five years old, but she appeared very official in her uniform. She wore a white blouse with a deep-red vest and a pine-green tie. The name Eve was etched into her gold name tag. She offered Ansley a smile. "Are you ready?"

Ansley shook her head. "We're missing my escort. He should be—"

"Right here." Zane's breathless statement came from behind Eve. He darted around her and came to stand at Ansley's side. He brushed a kiss to her temple and murmured, "Sorry I'm late." His hand slipped around her waist, which only exacerbated the fluttering of her heart.

It had only been one week since she and Zane had been thrown together at this resort, and already, her life had changed drastically. There was no telling what would happen over the course of the next several months.

For all she knew, it could go either way. They could end up together, just like Kate and Liam. Or they might finally realize that long-term relationships weren't something they could ever succeed at.

But as she leaned into him, twisting her head to find him smiling down at her, somehow, she knew it was the former. Zane was the only man who'd been able to help her realize just how much she was missing.

Ansley glanced up to find Eve staring at them. She shifted within Zane's arm and looked away briefly. When she returned her focus to the wedding attendant, the woman smiled broadly. "You two make such a beautiful couple. How long have you been together?"

Ansley stiffened. It was still strange to have someone make a comment like that. But more than that, it bordered on embarrassing. The short amount of time didn't explain how close they had become. She still didn't believe in love at first sight. The temptation to lie through her teeth was strong, but Zane beat her to the punch.

"You know? It feels like we've been together forever, and at the same time, we haven't been together nearly long enough."

It was the perfect response—one more reason that Zane was the perfect guy for her. She smiled at him and rested her head against his chest. She'd been wound far too tight for far too long. It was time to let loose, even if it was just a little.

Eve sighed. "That's so sweet." She nodded in Kate's direction. "I knew they were destined to be together from the first moment I saw them on the mountain."

Ansley's brows furrowed. "What?"

Eve nodded. "Sure. Last year, those two had the hardest time getting along, but they were forced together for an event. It was a couples' retreat if I'm remembering correctly." She snickered and leaned in closer. "Secretly, I take all the credit for getting them together. That retreat was the only way they would have met."

Ansley stared at the woman, her mouth hanging slightly open.

Eve noticed her shock and laughed again. "Let's just say I have a sense about these things. I can tell just by looking at a couple that they're going to make it work." She tilted her head as her focus bounced from Zane to Ansley. "Just like I can tell that the two of you are going to be just fine." She turned on her heel and headed in Kate's direction.

"That was sorta weird, wasn't it?" Ansley stared after the strange woman. "There's no way she'd have that kind of wisdom. She can't be any older than I am. In fact, I would bet she's younger by at least a year."

Zane moved until he stood in front of her. He grasped her chin with his finger and thumb, dragging her gaze from the woman to his eyes. Those dark eyes that seemed to see right through her and could communicate a hundred things in just one look. She shivered as a chill raced down her spine.

He smiled and cocked his head slightly. "You know what I think? I think that woman has probably seen more than her fair share of relationships. I would wager that she's seen them fail and she's seen them succeed. And"—he tapped her nose with his finger—"she's probably gotten pretty good at seeing a pattern."

Ansley frowned. "No two relationships are the same. We've seen evidence of that more times than we could probably count."

"True. No two relationships are the same, but the way two people seem to look at each other when they're in love tends to be the same."

She made a noncommittal sound. "Meh, I wouldn't agree with that, either."

He tossed back his head and laughed. "Why can't you just give this to me?"

There was no way she could hide the smile on her face. The way he made her feel was like nothing she'd ever experienced before, and she wasn't about to water it down with some mumbo-jumbo blanket statement.

His eyes found hers again. "You're not going to make this easy, are you?"

Her smile widened as the one-word answer she'd given to this exact question escaped her lips for a second time that week. "*Never.*"

Zane cupped her cheek with his hand and traced his thumb along her cheek. "Ansley, I—"

The music changed, growing into a crescendo, and the crowd of people sitting on either side of the aisle rose. Zane looked over his shoulder and then back to her, his eyes filled with an intensity she couldn't read. He opened his mouth again, as if he was prepared to continue the statement he was just about to make, but Eve materialized at his side.

"*Go.* You're on."

"But I—"

She turned him around and pulled him to stand beside Ansley then grabbed her hand to loop it through his arm while muttering, "I don't get paid nearly enough for this. Everyone else finds love, and I'm stuck here, helping them move through the fog of romance, desire, rose petals, and magical animals."

Ansley snickered, pulling her bouquet to her face as she shot Zane a sheepish smile. There was no way he hadn't heard what she'd said.

However, his expression remained straight and serious. He mouthed the words *I love you*.

Her stomach flipped, and her legs went weak. This was everything she had never known she wanted and more.

Eve gave them both a gentle push, and they strode down the aisle side by side.

He held her heart now, and that was perfectly okay.

"I love you too," she murmured.

Epilogue

O ne year later

Zane paced in the back room behind the reception desk. Metal shelving lined both sides of the small closet, filled with various items. Boxes of forgotten belongings and things held for safekeeping filled every square inch of the room. He should have known better than to let the hotel keep track of the small velvet box. "What do you mean you can't find it? I told you I wanted you to keep it safe."

"It's just like I told you, sir. It's not here."

The man's name tag was partially blocked, but when he turned, Zane could see in black lettering the word Gabriel. He had sandy hair, and his golden-brown eyes nearly matched it. He frantically moved small objects around on the shelving unit and continued shooting concerned looks at Zane.

Raking a frustrated hand through his hair, Zane

moved closer, causing the man to jump back. "Are you sure you didn't put it somewhere... safer? I'm sure when I brought it up here, they took it to a room with a safe."

Gabriel shook his head. "This room locks. If it was a short-term hold, it'd be here." He pushed aside another box, forcing a few objects too close to the edge and causing them to tumble to the ground.

One cardboard box tipped onto its side, and a small red velvet object skittered across the floor. Zane lunged for it, relief flooding his entire being. His shaking hands flipped open the lid to reveal the ring he'd picked out for Ansley.

It had to be perfect like her.

And it had to show how dedicated he was to her.

A sigh burst from behind his right shoulder, and he turned to find Gabriel breathing heavily, the relief on his face matching his own. "It's a beautiful piece."

"I know."

Gabriel stepped back, holding open the door to the lobby. The soft melody of "Silent Night" drifted into the storage room as they passed through the doorway. "She's a lucky girl."

Zane's lips twitched at the corners. "No. *I'm* the lucky one."

Gabriel smiled. "I totally get that." His focus shifted across the room, where a familiar woman with dark hair and green eyes stood beside a large Christmas tree. She held a clipboard and a pen.

Zane's gaze drifted from the woman back to Gabriel. "Have you asked her out yet?"

Gabriel's eyes grew round, and he sliced his hand through the air dismissively. "Eve would never go out with me. We're just friends—*work* friends."

"She'll never know you like her if you don't say anything about it." Zane nudged the guy with his elbow. "That first attempt is the hardest one. After that—"

"That's just it. If I ask her out and she says no, I don't get another shot."

Zane laughed. "That's not true. I'm pretty sure a lot of people just need a push in the right direction. Go talk to her. You miss all the shots you don't take... and all those corny words of encouragement."

Gabriel shoved his hands into his pockets and shook his head. "Nah. I don't want to make things weird."

Zane shrugged. "Suit yourself. I've got dinner reservations and a girl to make mine." He tossed the ring box into the air and caught it with one hand. "Thanks for helping me find this." He nodded toward Eve. "And good luck with that."

He hurried toward the elevator. It had taken months of planning and coordinating with the resort to make tonight happen. They'd leave by Christmas, because her mother wouldn't stand for a second year of not seeing her daughter, but they could stay up until Christmas Eve, and he fully planned to capitalize on every second of it.

Fingering the box in his hand, he fought to keep his heart rate from accelerating too much. They'd both come far from the people they had been when they'd been here for Kate and Liam's wedding. Now it was their turn to make this place special.

The elevator doors opened, and he stepped inside. If everything was as it should be, the ballroom would be decorated with ambient lighting. There would be red rose petals on the floor. And there would be one single table in the center, set with her favorite food.

Hopefully, she wasn't there yet. Ansley should arrive after he'd gotten situated beside the table. He glanced at his watch and shook his head. The elevator was moving too slowly. He should have taken the stairs.

When the doors opened, he jumped out and ran down the hall toward the ballroom. He burst into the room and skidded to a stop.

Ansley stood about ten feet from the door, her back facing him. She wore a slinky red dress that came to the floor. The two straps on her shoulders dipped low in the back, showing off her skin. It wasn't something she'd wear outside, but it was perfect for the season.

And he had a sinking suspicion that she'd known about this little dinner.

Slowly, she turned toward him, her hair curled in waves and resting on her shoulder. Zane sucked in a breath and placed his hand on his heart. Her eyes shone, and her jaw trembled. "Zane?"

In two long strides, he was beside her and taking her hand in his. "You're early."

Ansley let out a watery laugh and shook her head.

"Maybe you're just late." She motioned to the table, where two place settings had been laid along with two wine glasses. "What's this?"

His focus landed on the table briefly before returning to her. "You are so beautiful."

She tilted her head, a soft smile touching her lips. "Thank you."

"And I love you *so much*." His voice broke. Zane cleared his throat and slowly lowered himself to one knee. He still held her hand in his, and he brought it to his lips. "There's no one I'd rather spend the rest of my life with than you."

She sucked in a breath, and her eyes brimmed with emotion.

"Neither one of us has had very good examples set for us when it comes to relationships."

"Zane—" she whispered.

"But I know we're strong enough to carve our own path."

"Zane"—she laughed—"just spit it out already." Her voice shook, and she fidgeted. "I don't think I can endure a long speech with the way my legs feel like they're turning into Jell-O."

He dropped his eyes to the ground and chuckled. "You've never been very patient."

"Speak for yourself."

"Will you let me finish?" The humor blended with the exasperation in his voice.

She tugged on his hand as if to pull him to his feet,

but he refused to budge. "Come on, Zane. You don't have to be down—"

"No. I'm doing this my way." He studied her face, marveling at everything he'd managed to win in his life. "You deserve everything, and I'm going to do whatever I can to make that happen." He pulled the ring box out and flipped it open.

Ansley gasped, and the smile fled from her face.

"I love you *so much*, Ansley. Nothing would make me happier than to make you mine—forever. I know we can get through anything as long as we're together. Promise me that you'll be my wife."

She squeezed her eyes shut, and a tear slipped down her cheek as she nodded. "I promise."

He slipped the ring onto her finger and got to his feet in time for her to throw her arms around his neck and bury her face in his shoulder. Zane slipped his arms around her waist and pulled her tight against him.

Ansley pulled back, framing his face in both of her hands. "I love you more than you can imagine. I'm so lucky I found you."

He chuckled. "Actually, I'm the lucky one."

Come Back to Sweet Paradise Resort

Grab another cup of hot chocolate and cozy up with the next Sweet Paradise Resort holiday romance.

He's loved her since the first day they met, but she's more interested in helping others find their happily ever after.

Eve has spent her young adult life playing matchmaker for the guests at Sweet Paradise Resort. Just because she hasn't found love yet doesn't mean she's doomed to live alone, does it? Besides, she has other priorities. One day, she's going to be the events manager at the resort, and nothing is going to stop her.

Gabriel can't remember a day when he didn't have feelings for Eve. She's always been his bright light in an otherwise dim world. Eve doesn't know about his feelings, but she will soon because he's finally going to do it. He's going to ask her out.

But before he gets his chance, Eve insists on setting Gabriel up with someone who would be perfect for him. There's just one problem. Seeing him with someone does something strange to her heart.

Has she made the biggest mistake of her life? Can she get up the courage to admit there is no one else she'd rather be with?

Christmas Cookies and Coworkers is available for purchase at www.hopeaugust.com and select book retailers.

Paperback, large print, and book bundles are available at www.hopeaugust.com

Also by Hope August

Sweet Paradise Resort Christmas

Saving Paradise Resort (series prequel)

Christmas Honeymoon (For One)

Christmas Cookies and Coworkers

Maid for Mistletoe Mix-up

A Sweet Paradise Holiday Reunion

Sagebrush Dude Ranch Christmas

Snowfall Over Sagebrush (series prequel)

Mistletoe Masquerade

Gingerbread Hearts

Beneath the Christmas Star

Tinsel Trail

Crossroads at Sagebrush

Visit www.hopeaugust.com to purchase these and other new releases by Hope August.

About the Author

Hope August lives in central Texas with her family, which includes two chihuahua mix rescues. She loves reading romance stories with all the feels and creating characters you might recognize in real-life.

One more thing...

If you enjoyed this story, please consider sharing your thoughts with other readers so they can enjoy it, too. Leave an honest review at www.hopeaugust.com or anywhere this book is sold.

Thank you!

BB bookbub.com/authors/hope-august